The

Peacemaker

His Searchers

Book 1

By

Ronna M. Bacon

Matthew 5:9

Blessed are the peacemakers, For they shall be called sons of God. (NKJV)

John 14:27

Peace I leave with you, My peace I give to you; not as the world gives do I give to you. Let not your heart be troubled, neither let it be afraid.

Table of Contents

Chapter 1

His police-issue revolver held in both hands and pointed downwards, Flynn Brophy nodded at the patrol officer waiting beside him, motioning with his chin towards the door in front of them. Storm, as he was affectionately known as, paused for a moment to pray, not knowing what he and Tad faced on the other side of the door. A call had come in to the emergency dispatch, simply stating that armed men had entered an office and were holding the people inside hostage.

Crouching low as they crept through the door, Storm and Tad searched, puzzled looks on their faces as they didn't find anyone in the office at the back of the building. Storm knew the building from his undercover, street cop days. There were always people in here.

Hearing the sound of loud voices, the men crept forward, standing on either side of a doorway. They exchanged looks at the loud voice, recognizing it as coming from one of the owners of the office.

Storm frowned as he listened to the words. Something was off, that much he knew. The owner of this business was not involved in any crime, or at least that was what he had understood. He would need to look into that, he thought, tucking it away to the back of his mind as he listened further.

Tad motioned towards the back of the office and Storm nodded. Tad was off, heading outside for his car and radio. He agreed with Storm's silent appraisal of the situation. Something was off and he wanted to know what.

Storm edged back from the edge of the door as he heard heavy footsteps heading his way and frowned once more. The man was not on his own, he could tell, hearing the lighter footsteps of a woman. He waited, watching carefully as the man entered the room, shoving the woman ahead of him. She barely kept her balance, spinning in anger to glare at the man, Storm's presence in the room catching at the edge of her vision.

Moving silently forward and with a few quick moves, Storm had the man down and handcuffed, the scarf handed him by the woman, no lady, he thought, gagging the man and quieting his words. A hand reached out for hers as Storm pulled her towards the door and safety. They ran for his car where he opened the door and shoved her inside, the door closing quietly behind her.

Tad approached, ducking his head to look at the lady, before looking back at Storm. Storm's red gold curls were ruffled, and Tad saw the trouble in his deep blue eyes.

"Storm?" Tad waited before he spoke again. "What happened?"

"The brute shoved her into the office. He would have disappeared with her, I think, or else shot her. He's down and cuffed." Storm gave a grim smile. "She's feisty, Tad. Didn't stay back at all. Instead, she handed me the scarf that she was wearing and I used it to gag him. Did they say how many?"

—

8

"There are three more in the office." The lady stood beside him, anger and fear on her face.

"What part of staying put don't you get?" Storm pointed to his car. "You're to stay in there."

"No, I won't. They threatened me and I want to know why." She glared at him, her brown eyes angry but also showing her deep fear. "I don't have any enemies. At least, I don't think that I do." She spun to stare at the building, her long golden blond hair flowing around her, fascinating Storm for a moment.

"That may be all well and good. Back in the car." When she refused to move, Storm's hand grasped her arm as he almost shoved her back in and shut the door, this time standing with his back against it.

"Do you really think that will keep her in there?" Tad was amused for a moment before he sobered. He listened to the chatter on the radio before he pointed at Storm. "Head in with her. The chief was around when you were still inside. He wanted us to bring in whoever it was that we could."

"I know. I just wish I knew why." Storm shrugged before he headed for the driver's side, sliding in, and starting the car. He studied his companion for a moment, watching with some amusement as she refused to look at him. "I'm heading into the detachment with you. We need to get your statement."

She snorted before she turned to him.

"There's not much to say. I didn't see them coming in or hear them. I was working away, doing transcription. You know, the work that you do with

—

9

earphones on?" She glared as Storm grinned at her. "He was there, grabbed my arm, yanked me to my feet, and then shoved me through that door. Where did you come from?"

"Someone called it in. Tad and I went in the back door. That's where you found me." Storm pulled to the side of the road, his phone out. He listened for a moment before he responded.

Sitting still, his fingers tapping at the steering wheel, Storm thought through the words from his chief. It should have been his supervisor on the plains clothes unit who called. Only he was tied up at the crime scene, waiting to move in. The chief had made a request which became an order. Storm was not to come into the detachment. Instead, he was to find somewhere safe for his witness. And only let the chief know where he was. That they had a leak somewhere, that went without saying. Otherwise that request would not have been made.

The lady stared at Storm and then through the windshield, puzzled for a moment.

"Don't you have to drive away from here?" She pointed a slim finger at the road. "Aren't we heading for the police station?"

Storm studied her for a moment.

"No, we're not. First, I need to know your name."

"My name? It's Teagan Connell. Why?"

"I need to know your name as you are now a protected witness."

"Protected witness?" Teagan stared at him before she snorted. "Not likely, buster."

Storm stared at her in turn. Did she really just do that? And say that?

"Yes, a protected witness. My chief asked me to take you somewhere safe and keep you there until he can reach out to me."

"Why?" Teagan was confused. This was not how they did it or at least that is what she thought.

"Because he has word that someone has a contract out on you. As in to kill you. Why that is? We don't know." Storm knew that his street friends and sources would be working their best. As soon as they knew that he was involved, there would be no hesitation. He had seen Old Bill watching him drive away and knew word would get out right away.

"So? Somewhere safe? And just where would that be?" Teagan was not backing down.

"I'll find somewhere. I know lots of places." He stared at her for a moment. "Only it means that you will have to change into grubby clothes."

"Grubby clothes? I don't think so." Teagan stared out the window.

"Grubby clothes. So will I. Look, Teagan, we're not doing this for fun. Someone wants to kill you. We need to find who that is and why. And I need to keep you safe. I worked undercover for years on these streets. Going to grubby clothes means that I can take us to the streets and work that way to keep you safe. They'll be looking for our safe houses, the hotels and motels that we usually use. This will throw them off." He sighed. "This isn't up for discussion. It's happening." He drove away, heading for a source to find them those very clothes.

An hour later, Teagan stared at herself in the mirror of the home that Storm had brought to. *Lord, what is happening? This doesn't feel right, but I trust him.* It has to be You doing this. The grubby clothes that Storm had found her consisted of ragged jeans, an oversized sweatshirt, sneakers that he rubbed dirt into, and a hat that he had made her tuck her hair under. She studied him, taking in the grubby jeans and T-shirt, worn sneakers, and bandanna that he had tied around his head. She wouldn't have recognized him, she thought.

Storm watched closely, knowing that she was uncomfortable in her clothes, uncertain as to whether she could trust him, and more than likely deeply afraid. He simply shouldered the backpack he had stuffed food and whatnot into and reached for her hand. His friend nodded, taking the keys to the car, and closed the door after them. *Be with them,* the pastor of the mission Storm favoured, Rogan Fitzgerald, prayed. *Keep them safe. I have no idea what Storm is facing but You do. He is trying so hard to be that peacemaker for You but this will drive him back to the streets and the danger there. His street name is Storm, in contrast to Your peace that he shows in all situations.*

Chapter 2

Teagan's hand tight in his, Storm headed for the downtown streets. Teagan was puzzled. This was not how she expected a protected witness to be handled. Not at all. She kept glancing at Storm, finding his head moving as he searched the area.

At last, he dropped to a park bench, pulling her down with him. She sighed, her feet sore from the walk.

"Is this how you treat your protected witnesses?" Teagan's voice was sarcastic. She just couldn't help herself.

"No, not usually." Storm was listening to her, hearing the underlying fear in her voice that she was trying hard to cover up. "We usually take them into the detachment and then to a safe house. Only, for some reason, we can't do that with you."

"And that would be because?" Teagan could feel the anger rising in her, anger driven by her fear.

"Because somewhere there's a leak. We have to find out who and that takes time. You're stuck with me for now." Storm spared her a look before his eyes roamed once more. "And it's not going to be easy or very nice for you."

"I didn't expect it to be. Only I need to be at home tomorrow."

"Not happening." Storm's hand tightened on hers, keeping her in her seat.

"But I have to. I have a family dinner to give." She sighed, her brow furrowed. "Guess that's not happening. Is that what you're saying?"

"That's it exactly." He handed her his phone, having made her leave hers with Rogan. "Text them, tell them it's off, and that you'll be in touch. That you're safe." He kept shoving the phone at her until she took it. "You have to get word to at least one of them. It will be all over the news what happened at your work. Don't you think that they'll be worried?"

"I know my brother and sister will be. My parents are away right now, not expected back for a month." Teagan stared at his phone. "They won't answer. Not knowing the number."

"Then send a text message stating it's from you and that you're under police protection." His hand folded over hers as he prayed for her, causing her to raise her head to stare at him.

Somehow, Teagan thought, *this is not how they do this. I have never heard of a police officer praying for a witness. But then, again, maybe they do and just don't say it.*

Storm's senses brought his head up before he was on his feet, pulling Teagan with him. He searched, finding an alcove to tuck her away in, his body in front of hers, back to the sidewalk. *It didn't take them long,* he thought, *to go to the streets and search for her. Now, how do we do this?* He turned slightly as he heard a soft sound.

———

Old Bill stood with his back to Storm, watching the two men stomp down the street. That they were angry, he understood only too well. He had seen them around and at one point, had felt their anger directed at him.

"Storm? I don't know what you've gone and gotten involved in but you're back here on the streets. Those two mean you and your lady harm. I'm set up in the Hardy building. Head there. We'll cover your going." Old Bill walked away without waiting for Storm to answer but then he knew Storm wouldn't reply. Not and give away his location.

Storm shifted his body to watch up the street, seeing the men disappear. He could hear muttering coming from Teagan and smiled grimly. Yes, she was upset and had every right to be, but if keeping to the streets kept her alive, then that's what he would do. He just wasn't comfortable dragging her around with him. Not as a single man or a single lady. That went against his beliefs and personal convictions.

Teagan was tired of running. Storm had kept her on the move the whole afternoon, she thought. The fright from the morning was weighing her down as was a lack of food and drink. She tugged at his hand, bringing them to a stop.

Storm turned, a frown on his face before it cleared. He studied the whiteness of Teagan's face and the black shadows that were appearing under her eyes. He needed to get her to somewhere she could rest and have something to eat. Old Bill would provide for them, that much he knew. He had handed him money when Old Bill had stopped, something

—

15

that he had done in the past. He knew that food and water at the very least would be waiting for them.

"In here, Teagan. We'll rest and have something to eat." He tugged her with him through the broken door and into a room at the back of the building.

Teagan was too tired to take in much of the room. She sank down gratefully on the blanket that Storm had led her to. She found a blanket, shook it out, and then wrapped herself in it. It surprised her that it was clean, given the state of the building. A somewhat decrepit bench beckoned to her and she slumped on it, her eyes barely able to stay open.

Storm watched her closely, a sigh rising within him. The incessant vibrating of his phone caught his attention and he pulled it out. It was the chief, simply stating that Storm was to stay away from the building and to stay safe. He would be in touch as he could. Things were heating up regarding his witness and they needed to ensure that she would be safe. Keeping her safe? Storm shook his head. That would be a task in itself, he decided. He knew that he could go to Rogan if he needed to and he would help them to hide. So would Old Bill and his friends on the streets. He just had to convince Teagan that was the best for them. And that? Storm had a good idea of just how difficult that would be.

Chapter 3

Old Bill watched from the shadows, his eyes on Storm before they shifted to Teagan. He was very concerned, to say the least, hearing the scuttlebutt on the street. He had taken a walk past Teagan's workplace and had news for Storm, news that he didn't think Storm would like to hear. And he just knew that Teagan would be frightened. That was unavoidable.

Storm turned, his fists up and ready to defend Teagan before his hands dropped. Old Bill just shook his head before he handed over the bag of food that he was carrying. He had stopped at the mission and Rogan had beckoned him over, a bag of hot food and beverages changing hands.

"Rogan sent it." Old Bill dropped to the floor near Teagan, causing her to jump in fear. "It's okay, little lady. I'm a friend. I have food here for you." He shared a look with Storm. "And then we have to talk."

"Talk? About what?" Teagan was just too tired at that point to really care. She accepted the styrofoam container of food as well as the bottle of water, watching as the two men bowed their heads as Storm asked a blessing on their food. *This is interesting,* she thought to herself. *Both of them? I wouldn't have thought.* Then, Teagan sighed to

—

17

herself. She was judging these two without any basis to do so.

Storm gathered the debris from their meal, trying to come up with a plan that didn't mean keeping Teagan on the street. It just wasn't working.

"Storm?" Old Bill's voice drew him back, to a sitting position beside Teagan, who frowned at him. "We need to talk."

"We do. You've been around there?" Storm had no doubt that he had been.

"I have. It's not pretty, Storm. All of them are dead. The owner, the receptionist, the salesman. The man that you tied up? He's disappeared. The three that were in the main office? Gone. Tad? He was at the back door. He's in hospital, in critical condition."

Teagan's face had paled even more as Old Bill spoke, turning towards Storm.

"That's about what I thought you'd have to say. The chief wants me away from the detachment. Only, I don't know that we can stay on the streets for long. Teagan's not used to it." Storm was running scenarios through his mind, trying to come up with a plan.

"They are?" Teagan was horrified. "Why?"

"That's what they're working on." Storm had checked his voice mail earlier and then shut his phone off. He needed to preserve the battery charge until he could get a charger and then charge it. "I have taken your statement and sent it on. The chief is the only one with it."

"He is?" Teagan shook in fear for a moment. "They're looking for me, aren't they? I just don't understand why."

"I don't either. The chief will keep me up to date. I'm not leaving my phone on all the time." Storm just shook his head. "I need to move you tonight. Old Bill and I will come up with a plan and a place."

Teagan sank back, her eyes sliding closed. "I'm tired, Storm. Can I sleep for a bit before you start dragging me all over creation?"

Storm stared at her, his mouth open, even as he heard Old Bill chuckling.

"We can do that. Teagan, just be prepared to move and move quickly. If I say run, you do that." Storm waited until he saw her nod and then doze off.

Old Bill shook his head at her before he began to speak.

Storm finally nodded.

"I know, Old Bill. I have to get out of here. I need to get back to the detachment and retrieve my car. From there, I can head home, find what I need, and then take off."

"I know that you need to do that. Let her sleep for an hour and then we'll head off. If I'm with you, it will be less obvious than the two of you on your own." It would not be the first time that Old Bill had done that.

Chapter 4

Standing in the shadows, Old Bill held a position that would shield Teagan from sight. They had stopped near a large oak tree, and Storm had simply told her to stand behind it and wait for him. He pointed towards the detachment.

"I'm going in there, getting my personal vehicle, and then we're leaving." His eyes had held a touch of amusement as Teagan opened her mouth to protest and then snapped it closed, a glare heading his way. "Lose the attitude, Teagan. This isn't fun for any of us, trying to find out what's going and then keeping you alive. Both Old Bill and I are putting our lives on the line for you." He was away, running across the street in the early twilight and then disappearing from sight.

Storm keyed in his code, slipped through the gates and then to his car. He searched it thoroughly even though it had been locked up in their parking area. He just had a bad feeling about it all.

Slipping away without being seen, other than on the security cameras, Storm pulled to a halt near the oak tree, watching as Old Bill headed his way, opening the front passenger's door and shoving Teagan in before he quietly shut the door and disappeared into the night. Storm pulled away, with just a quiet word to Teagan to fasten her seatbelt.

—

Teagan studied Storm as best she could in the dim light from the dashboard and in the flashes of light from the street lamps. She was puzzled. She had no idea where they were heading but she trusted him.

"I'm heading for my home, Teagan. I had someone do some shopping for you, given that you can't go home. They also stopped by to see Rogan and retrieved your phone." Storm's eyes were in constant movement even as he shot a quick glance at Teagan.

Teagan simply nodded, knowing that it had to be that way but not liking it one bit. *Lord, I'm sorry. I know Storm is trying to keep me safe. Only I can't do this. I can't run and hide. That's not me. I need to be out front, defending myself. It's what I've had to do all my life.*

"Teagan?" Storm was worried, to say the least. He didn't know how to proceed and that was unlike him.

"It's okay, Storm. Do what you need to. I just don't have to like it." She refused to look at him.

"Teagan, that's what we're trying to do. But you need to work with us. If you can't, then I take you to my chief. He'll lock you up somewhere and you won't have any freedom. None whatsoever. With me, you'll have a certain amount."

"But how do you do this?" Teagan finally shifted, to study him as best she could.

"We make plans, Teagan, more than one. We may need to leave town to keep you safe. I have areas and friends that I can go to."

—

"But that would put your friends at risk." She frowned as he grinned. "Storm?"

"It's okay. The friends that I would go to? All retired or mostly retired officers my age. All of them have had what we term as adventures, life and death situations. They will work to keep us safe."

"You too? You're not in danger." Teagan gaped at him for a moment before snapping her mouth shut.

"Me, too, Teagan. Just by being the one who got you away and is keeping you hidden? That makes me a target." He stopped his car down the street from his house, studying it. "I think it's okay if we go in. Through the garage. Duck down for a moment until I pull in and get the door back down."

Teagan wandered through Storm's home, liking what she saw. It's peaceful, she thought. A refuge from the sorrow and sadness that he sees in his work. She had showered and changed to more comfortable clothes. Teagan had stared down at the pile of clothes, wonder on her face. Whoever had shopped for her had almost nailed perfectly her choices of clothes and colour.

Storm stood in the doorway to his kitchen. He had pulled a meal from the freezer and started his coffee. Teagan had shrugged when he had asked what she liked to drink, not committing to anything. He sighed at that, knowing that at some point, she would talk with him. He had prepared sandwiches and packed them into a cooler along with bottles of juice and water. Fruit had been added as well. That they would be on the move was a given. They

—

couldn't stay here. He had turned on his phone long enough to speak with the chief. Will Peters had been blunt. Storm had been made and whoever it was that had committed the crime was on the look out for him. He didn't want to know exactly where they were, just that they were safe. Storm had promised to check in once a day, more if needed. Will had simply stated that Storm needed to check his voice mail on a regular basis.

Chapter 5

Her face turned away from Storm, Teagan stared out the side window of his car, into the dark, broken only by the light of the street lamps that passed by the moving vehicle. She was tired, she decided, tired and worn out. Today had been brutal in more ways than one. It was a day that she just wanted over so that she could return to her home, lock the doors and lock out the world. Only, it wasn't happening. Teagan had no idea where she was heading at the moment. Storm hadn't said, she thought, if he even knew where he was going.

Storm's eyes were in constant movement, searching for whoever it was that was after Teagan. And who that was he had no idea. Will had not offered a lot of information when they had spoken an hour earlier. Either because he couldn't or because he didn't know, not yet anyway. Storm thought it was likely the latter. The investigation would only be in the early stages. He prayed that Davy Smithson would be brought in as the investigator. He was a fellow street cop returning to the detachment as an investigator not long before Storm had come onto the plains clothes squad.

He eyed Teagan on occasion, a slight smile on his face that held sadness. What had she gotten involved in, he wondered? And how did it affect him? *Lord,* he prayed, *I have no idea where we're heading. You called me to be Your peacemaker, to*

---

turn people to You and to Your peace. Only it doesn't seem to be working out all that well. How do I do this? How do I keep this witness safe?

Glancing over at Teagan once more as he drove through the outskirts of his town, Storm sighed and then pulled into a parking lot, seeking an out of the way spot to stop in. He reached behind him for a small pillow. Tucking it under her head, his hand rested for a moment on her cheek. She had not roused as he had lifted her head, fatigue driving her to sleep. A blanket was reached for next before he shook it out and then tucked it around her.

Storm studied the parking lot. It was empty almost, he thought, other than for a few cars likely belonging to security, cleaners and night staff. It was a parking lot that he had often come to, knowing he would find or leave information as the case may be.

He shifted in his seat, his back against the door, as his own eyes closed. He would sleep for a bit, he knew, and then be awake to move once more. But just where to? That was the question. He needed to speak with Will. Only that wouldn't happen until morning. Will he knew would not leave his office during these early hours of the investigation. Sadness seeped through him at the lives lost. His prayer was for those families and also for Tad. How serious Tad was? That he needed to find out.

Two hours later, Storm was wide awake, his senses working overtime. He keyed the motor to life and pulled away from the parking lot, watchful for anyone out of place. He didn't see anyone but his street senses were warning him that someone was there. Teagan had awakened as the vehicle moved, her eyes moving as she did so, searching for just who, she wasn't sure.

Storm pulled into another parking lot, his phone out and turned on, listening to his voice mail. It had gotten worse, he thought. Will had called just after midnight, warning Storm that he likely needed to leave town. Whoever it was that was after Teagan was searching for her. Word had gotten to him from Old Bill that they were searching the streets, offering good money for her whereabouts. Only no one had taken them up on that, as yet.

He sighed, his eyes on Teagan. *Where, Lord, do we go? Who do I turn to? Will would not be sending me out of town unless he had good reason. I need to speak with him at some point today. Only I won't use my phone.*

"Storm?" Teagan's voice broke through the silence. "What are we waiting for? Don't you have to take in me or something?" She was disgruntled and afraid and those emotions came through in her voice.

"No, I can't. Will has asked that I take you out of town somewhere. Only I don't know where." He turned to face her, finding her staring at him, her mouth open.

Teagan began to shake her head, disbelief on her face.

"That's not happening. I'm going home. I'll walk if you don't take me." Her hand reached for the door handle even as his hand clamped down tight on her arm. "What are you doing?"

"I am repeating myself. You are a protected witness. You're not walking anywhere on your own." Storm bit at his lip even as his eyes narrowed. "You can't."

"And why not? I'm refusing your protection."

"That's not happening, Teagan. I spoke with Will before you awoke." He hesitated, his face becoming even more grim. "Your family has been threatened and Will has had to take steps to protect them. You will not know where they are for now. Your home? It burnt overnight."

"My house? That can't be right." Teagan sat back, shock wafting through her body. "No, that can't be right. How did they know where I lived?"

"Easy. They watched you and followed you. This is not some random event, Teagan. It was planned. We need to keep you safe as we work through this. And until we get to a point where you're safe on your own, you're stuck with me." Storm shook his head at her. "No, you're not out there on your own."

Teagan blinked rapidly, devastation striking at her. She hadn't owned the house, not yet. She was working through that with the landlord, trying to come to a price that they could agree on. Now, that wouldn't happen. And he would blame her, that she was sure of.

"So, where do we go?" Her voice was really quiet and uncertain. Storm had finally managed to get through to her that she was in danger.

—

Chapter 6

Pulling to a stop at a curb, Storm stared at the remnants of the house. He heard the shocked sound from Teagan before he turned to look at her. She had demanded that he drive by her home, not quite believing him that it was destroyed.

"Teagan? We can't stay here. We'll get you back here at some point. But for now, we're on the move."

Teagan nodded, unable to see clearly for the tears that clouded her eyes. She sighed, knowing that he was right but she had a fiery, feisty side to her that was coming out. She was not willing or ready just to sit back and be taken care of. That was not her.

"Okay, I know that. But where do we go?" She turned to him when he didn't respond.

Storm sat, his hand on the gear shift, not sure where to head. He had briefly pulled up his voice mail, with no new messages. That worried him, he had to admit. Will should have been in touch.

"I'm not sure, Teagan. I can take you out to the Foundation building and hide you there for a couple of days. Or we head out of town and to friends of mine who will help."

"The Foundation building? I don't get that. They're not involved, are they?"

—

Storm gave a quick grin before he shifted to drive and did just that, driving away from her destroyed home, eyes watchful for anyone following him.

"Yes, the Foundation building. They would help us but I'm not sure that is the step we should take."

"Can we go somewhere that we can research all this?" Teagan was tired and just wanted to find a new home, one that she could set up once more.

"We can. But it means a bit of a drive." Storm headed for the highway and set out, heading north on it before he pulled off onto a secondary road.

"Storm?   Just where are we heading?" Teagan's head was turning as she searched the area, not recognizing it.

"To a friend's. Shay will help, I know. And we have other friends that will help as well. We'll do our best to keep you safe until we can solve this." He shot her a quick glimpse, not liking the look on her face. "Teagan? No running away on your own."

She finally gave an abrupt nod, determining to do just that. Teagan knew it would be difficult to elude Storm but she was determined to do just that, at some point. Her eyes closed as she tried to pray but just couldn't put into words what she was feeling. She also knew that she needed to find God's peace in what she was going through but was uncertain just how to do that.

Storm eventually pulled to a stop in front of a house in a town that Teagan didn't recognize or even know the name for. She studied him and then the house, sighing. *What has he gotten me into,* she wondered?

"Teagan. This is a friend's house. Shay and Breckon went through some really bad stuff. They had an adventure, as we term it, that almost killed them. Breckon would be a good one for you to speak with, if you want."

Teagan finally nodded, watching as a man walked towards the car. She frowned. He looks familiar but he can't be.

Storm was out of the vehicle, a hand outstretched to greet Shay before they stood talking. Breckon approached when they didn't head for the house, a hug given to Storm before she headed for Teagan.

"Hi. I'm Breckon. Won't you come on in?" Breckon waited for Teagan to move before she just hugged her and then arm around her, led her towards their home.

"This is nice. A cabin in the woods?" Teagan was curious about that.

"Absolutely. We found it just after we married and are working at making it ours, little by little. Storm won't say but Shay was undercover for many years. I worked as a proofreader but am still trying to determine what I want to do now." She watched Teagan closely, knowing that she had to have a story and just why had she appeared there with Storm. Storm was not dating, that much she knew.

Storm watched the ladies walk for the cabin before he sighed. This was likely a bad idea, he thought.

"Storm?" Shay turned as well, watching as Breckon turned to look at him before she closed the door. "What's going on? You're showing up here with a lady? You're not dating, not that we know of."

Storm shook his head, his eyes troubled.

"No, I'm not, Shay. But she's in trouble. I don't know if the news made it this far but her boss and two other employees were murdered yesterday morning. She was being taken out by one of them towards the back door of the office. I was there as was Tad. I took the man out and then took her to safety. Will has asked me to keep her safe, preferably out of town. Tad was hurt in the interim."

"I heard some of it but not this." Shay blew out a breath. "You've come to us. Who else knows where you are?"

"Right now? No one. I just packed up and left early this morning. We spent the night in my car in a parking lot. I didn't dare stay at my home. I had taken her to the streets right away, but didn't feel safe keeping her there." Storm paused, his mind working as to the next steps. "I could have gone to the Barnabas Foundation and they would have done their best to help. But there are little ones in that building. I didn't feel right going there."

"No, you wouldn't." Shay pointed to the house, reaching for one of the duffel bags that Storm pulled from the trunk. "Do you have information at all?"

Storm shrugged. "Not that I know of. I need to call Will and touch base with him. He may have sent something to my email, which I haven't accessed as yet."

Standing in Shay's living room. Storm watched Teagan before he walked towards her. She backed away before he handed her the duffle bag with her clothing.

"Breckon won't mind if you clean up. I know that's what you would like to do." A compassionate look came over his face as she hesitated and then nodded, turning to follow Breckon.

"She's afraid, Storm." Shay watched as well.

"She's afraid. But she's also a fighter. I've had my hands full at times just trying to get her to follow me. I had to threaten to take her back to Will." Storm ran his hands through his hair, before he picked up his duffle bag and walked to the room Breckon had told him to use.

Shay simply reached to hug Breckon, knowing that she had questions. Only he didn't know if he had the answers that she was looking for. Not yet, anyway.

Chapter 7

Teagan raised her head from the pillow that she was using, a frown on her face. It was late afternoon, she could see from the shadows in the room and from the direction of the sunlight. She sighed. After her shower, her body had simply crashed. Teagan was not aware that Breckon had tapped at her door and peeked in, closing it behind her as she backed away. Her head shook at Storm as she stated that Teagan was asleep.

Storm had nodded and turned to walk away, pausing for a moment. He had had a thought earlier about who it was but that thought was now elusive. He sank into a deck chair on the dock, his eyes on the lake which was relatively calm that morning. Shay had watched and then walked towards him, a mug of coffee on the chair arm before he sat.

"Storm? What actually happened? Do you know?" Shay spoke at last, his eyes on his friend.

Storm shook his head. "Not really. We were asked to go into a business as there was a call for help. Tad and I went in the back door. He left for a few minutes and then a man came through with Teagan. I took him down, handcuffed him and Teagan gave me her scarf as a gag. I put her in my car, even though she didn't stay there. I spoke with Will, took off with her, and then took her to the streets. But that wasn't safe. I had a bad feeling

—

about that and headed home. We packed what we could and then took off. It's bizarre, Shay. The man I handcuffed disappeared. Tad was wounded, and right now? I'm not even sure how he is."

"That weighs on you, not to say the worry about Teagan." Shay nodded to himself as he saw a look cross Storm's face. He's found his lady, hasn't he, Lord? And it's up to us to keep her safe.

"It really does, Shay. I am out of the loop as to what is being investigated. Will has asked that of me." Storm's head went back as his eyes closed. "I need to sleep but I need to contact Will." His phone was out as he made his call, shaking his head as Shay went to rise. Shay settled back down, his eyes on Storm.

"Will?" Storm could hear noise over the air and frowned.

"Storm? Hold on a moment." Will walked outside and away from the detachment, finding a bench to sit on. "Okay. I'm away from there. Are you two safe?"

"We are, for now. I'm out of town."

"That's good. It's a mess, to put it mildly, Storm. I've sent documentation and information to your secure email. Read them. Talk to Teagan. It's worse than what we thought."

"It is?" Storm frowned, puzzled as to why Will would say that.

"It is. She was the target, just as we thought. We're trying to work through why but there has been a major leak here. I know who it is and am working with Davy and only Davy to find the evidence that we need." Will hesitated, not sure if he should name who it was.

Storm sighed once more and said a name, hearing the silence on the other end of the line.

"You're correct, Storm. And that hurts, big time."

"It would. Listen, I'm shutting down my phone again. I can access my voice mail and email where I am. Keep in touch, Will. If I need to head back that way, let me know."

"I will. Stay safe, you two." Will pocketed his phone, trouble on his face, turning his head as Davy Smithson, a detective on the force, sat beside him. "Davy?"

"I've arrested her, Will. She's not saying anything but she's running scared of whoever was paying her."

Will nodded, lost in thought for a moment. "And that's what we need to determine, isn't it? Any thoughts?"

Davy shrugged, thinking back to his days on the street and then the investigations that he had underway.

"I have an idea but I would rather not say until I have more evidence. If it's who I think it is, we've been after them for years. And leave it to Storm to have to be the one."

"I know. His faith is strong, Davy. That will get him through. He's left town."

"I thought he would." Davy stretched out his legs, his eyes closing for a moment as the sun hit his face. "He'll not say where he is until he has to. Can we reach him?"

"Voice mail. His phone is off unless he needs to use it. He can access his email as well."

"That's good." Davy rose, a hand rubbing at his cheek. "I'll leave a message for him to call me. I take it that we keep the number contacting him to a minimum."

"That we do." Will stood as well, his eyes on Davy. "For now, Davy, I want you on this and this only. I'll clear it with Stuart. He'll look after sorting out your other cases."

"Thanks, Will. That's what I was praying you would say." Davy walked away, spying Old Bill waiting for him.

Will watched him stop by Old Bill before he headed for his vehicle. He needed to talk with Barnabas Carey of the Barnabas Foundation about what they could do to help. He knew that Barnabas would without any hesitation. And not just because it was Storm, who had helped out Dallas and Deri. It was how the Foundation worked, providing encouragement to their community and its residents.

———

Chapter 8

Walking through the cabin, Teagan paused in the kitchen, a frown on her face. Her phone sat on the counter, a charger running to it. She hadn't remembered putting it there. She refused to reach for it, turning instead to the door and the outside. Storm paused as he walked towards her, watching her closely.

"Teagan?" He stopped in front of her.

Teagan jumped at his voice, glaring at him in anger.

"Just where did you come from? And just where are we again?" Teagan stared at him. When he didn't answer, she turned and stomped around the cabin.

Storm's head dropped as his eyes closed for a moment before he was after her. His hand on her wrist startled her and she began to fight him, struggling to release herself from his grip. Shay had followed, an amused look on his face for a moment. Storm simply swept her into a hug, not releasing her arm until he had one arm around her. He just knew that she would take off if he did.

Teagan fought to release herself from Storm's strong hug, unable to do so.

"Let me go!" She continued to fight him even as he simply lifted her from the ground and carried

—

her back into the cabin, Breckon holding open the door, barely able to contain her grin. "Put me down!"

Storm dropped her to her feet, a hand still on her wrist to keep her from moving away. He simply stood and stared at her, no expression on his face. He wouldn't let her walk away, that much he knew.

"Teagan! Enough already. This is no fun for us either."

Teagan still struggled, her eyes on him, before she drew a deep breath.

"Storm? Let me go? Please?" Teagan rubbed at her wrist when he did. She still stared at him, a puzzled look in her eyes for a moment.

"Teagan? We can't have you disappearing from sight like that. They may well have followed us and are just waiting for an opportunity to nab you and disappear with you. It's worse than what you even thought. You've been followed for the last couple of months."

Teagan shook her head. "No, that didn't happen. That only happens in books or movies." She continued to shake her head even as Storm nodded. "No, it can't be. I would have known."

"Not necessarily." Shay spoke up from where he had planted himself against the front door, determined to keep her in the cabin. "Most people who are followed don't know that they are. Even us as officers would have difficulty at times spotting exactly who it would have been."

Storm was nodding, Breckon commenting that Shay was correct.

———

"He's right, Teagan. As an undercover officer, I perfected how to track someone and to spot someone who was doing the same. It's not something the average person would pick up on, unless they were really obvious. From what Will told me, it's wasn't obvious."

Teagan wrapped her arms around herself, seeking confirmation from Shay and then turning to Breckon.

"Is that what happened with you two?"

"It was, Teagan. Shay was undercover for years, since his teens, and he still had trouble finding the ones tracking us." Breckon moved to hug Teagan, finding her shaking as she did so. "Storm just wants to keep you alive. You do know that, don't you?"

Teagan sighed as she stepped back, her eyes going back to Storm's.

"I know. It's just hard, you know? All of a sudden, I'm threatened, kidnapped, placed in custody, my home destroyed, and then I have to leave my town. And for how long? Can anyone tell me that?" Teagan stared at each one in turn before her hands flew up in the air and then she stomped away from them towards the bedroom that she was told to use.

Storm followed her, a hand on the doorframe as he watched her at the window.

"Don't even think about going out that window, Teagan. I'll handcuff you to me to prevent that." Storm waited for her to speak. "Work with us. We're trying to keep you alive. I have information that I need to go over with you and I would prefer that

—

to be today. Get over your mad." He walked away, not seeing her spin and stare after him, her mouth open to protest.

I can't do that, Lord. I have to run. Someone is after me and I need to find out who. She sank down on the bed, her eyes on the door, waiting for one of them to return. Teagan could hear quiet conversation in another part of the house. Her head bowed and she began to pray, to petition God for the peace that she needed and hadn't felt in months.

$$Chapter\ 9$$

Storm paced around the cabin early that evening. He was disturbed, to put it mildly. He had taken a look at the material that Davy had forwarded to him. *It's worse than I imagined,* Storm thought. *How do we keep Teagan safe? She's going to fight me on this, I know, and that doesn't help.* He grinned for a moment at her feistiness, knowing that he wanted to keep her as a friend when this was all over. He didn't realize that Teagan was beginning to wriggle her way into his heart.

Teagan watched him from her perch on the back deck steps, a mug of coffee in her hand, his sitting beside her. *What is he thinking,* she wondered? *He's upset. I wonder what he found out after spending so much time on the computer. And will he share with me at all?*

Storm paced back around the cabin, finding a place to sit beside Teagan. He took with thanks the mug of coffee that she had handed him. He wasn't sure that they were safe, not at all, and he didn't like putting Shay and Breckon at risk. And at risk was just what they were. Storm knew that they wouldn't refuse to help him, but anyone who had followed him or studied his habits would know that they were friends.

"Storm? Where do we go?" Teagan's voice was low. She was exhausted and didn't know how to go on, not at the present moment.

Storm tilted his head to study her, taking in the dark shadows under her eyes. He sighed to himself. *She's hurting, isn't she, Lord? And how do I help her?* He sipped from his mug before he rested it on his leg, his hands cradling the mug.

"Teagan, I can't and won't lie to you. You are in grave danger. I can tell you some of what Davy has dug up but some I can't. It has to stay within the investigation."

Teagan nodded. "That's fair, but what can you say? And my family? They're safe?"

"They are. Will made sure of that. I spoke with him about an hour ago. Davy's been in touch, leaving voice mail for me." Storm studied the sky before he looked back at her, compassion on his face. "Teagan, this is where it gets dangerous for you. They will be watching your family. We don't know if they can trace your phone or not. That's why we would ask that you not use it."

"But, Storm? I need to talk to them. I just need my Mom." Teagan blinked back tears, her emotions getting the better of her a moment.

"And you can. I'll let you use mine. But for now? This is where it gets hard for you. I need you to listen to me and not try and run. And that's exactly what you will do." Storm grinned at her for a moment.

Teagan stared at him, a frown on her face for a moment. *I know this man,* she thought. *He's the knight in my stories from when I was young. Mom described him almost perfectly. But that's not right. He's just here to protect me and then will move on.*

"Okay, so what do you need to tell me?" Teagan watched him closely, seeing his face shutter for a moment. "Storm, don't go undercover cop on me. You need to tell me. If you won't, I'm out of here." She waited for a moment and then started to shove herself to her feet. Storm's hand on her arm kept her in place.

"Don't run, Teagan. I meant it when I said I'd handcuff you. Your running from us only puts yourself and everyone else around you in danger. Do you get that?" He stared her down, seeing the fright on her face for a moment. "Okay, so this is what I can tell you.

"Your boss, the receptionist, and the secretary were killed. This happened after you disappeared. It was likely to ensure that they didn't describe the men. We have video footage of the men as they entered the office and left. Why they were after you? That we don't know as of yet. The officers have served search warrants and are working through them.

"There is not a lot of information about why as yet. Just bits and pieces that we need to put together. You said that you did transcription?"

"I did. Letters and reports. He consulted with many different people in different countries as well as here. His business had grown to the point that his regular secretary couldn't do that any more and I was hired about eighteen months ago." Teagan bit at her lip. "I don't remember anything in any of the letters

---

43

or reports that would have caused this. He and his wife belonged to our church." She sighed. "This is not helping."

"No, it's not." Storm sighed as he felt his phone vibrating and pulled it out. His face hardened as he read the text message. "Teagan, just what have you gotten involved in? Some of those reports? The investigators have your originals but the final report that was printed varies from that. These reports are ones for a company in our town."

"They do? Which company or can't you tell me?" Teagan was afraid suddenly, not sure what to think. All she knew was that she was on the run and not able to be around her family. That angered her.

"The Whitley Insurance Company." Storm watched her reaction closely.

"Whitley's? He just took them on as a client. I don't know why. He's never done that before. His work? He was a contact for people wanting information on insurance companies, investment companies, financial stuff." She paled even further. "White collar crime?"

"We don't know as yet. For now, we keep you here and safe. Only, I don't like putting Shay and Breckon at risk." Storm was on his feet, pulling Teagan to hers. "Did you unpack?"

"No, I didn't. I just stuffed everything back into the bag. Why?" She looked up at him, frowning at his height.

"We need to move, Teagan, and now." Storm pulled her at a rapid pace back into the cabin and then grabbing their bags, pulled her to his car. He shoved

---

her into it, shoved the bags into the trunk and then slid behind the wheel, taking off in a cloud of dust.

Teagan stared at him, her mouth open to yell at him when she heard his yell for her to duck down. She felt the car accelerate rapidly and her fear took over, leaving her shaking.

"Storm?"

"They found us, Teagan, and I have no idea how." His phone was out and tossed to her. "Find Shay's number and text him that we've left and why. Now, I have to find a place to stash you that's safe."

Storm's eyes flickered between the rear view mirror and the road in front of him. How did they find us, Lord? I need to keep this lady safe and that doesn't seem to be happening.

Chapter 10

Storm headed for a nearby town, knowing that he had a friend on the force there who would help. Brownie was a relatively new acquaintance but he shared a faith in God with Storm. They had worked together lately. Teagan just stared at him, her eyes huge, not sure what was going on or where he was heading. He certainly hadn't told her.

An exclamation from Storm had Teagan's head spinning around. She stifled a scream as she saw the large pickup truck edging up beside them and closer to Storm's car. *This is it, isn't it, Lord?* She closed her eyes, not wanting to see the moment of impact.

Storm had little room to maneuver. He shot a look at the truck and then at the road ahead of him. A quick look in his rear view mirror showed nothing behind him. Slamming on his brakes, he watched the truck pull ahead and then spun his wheel to head back the way that he had just come. Then, he spun his wheel again, heading towards Brownie's town, and then shot off onto a side road. He was desperate to get away, knowing that his life was likely on the line if he didn't. And who knew what would happen to Teagan if they were caught.

Teagan stared at him, her mouth open, before she looked behind them.

"There's no sign of them." She stared at Storm again. "Did you really just do that?"

46

"Do what?" Storm's full concentration was on getting her away and to safety.

"What you just did. Your driving. You are really dangerous on the roads, did you know that?"

Storm gave a quick grim smile.

"Not really. If there had been other traffic, he wouldn't have tried that and I wouldn't have done what I did. Now, to get you to safety." Storm's eyes were watching for somewhere that he could pull off and call Will. He shot into a parking lot and then around to the back of the buildings, backing into a parking spot near a dumpster.

His phone out, he quickly called Will. When he just reached Will's voice mail, he tried Davy.

"Davy? It's Storm." Storm could hear Davy rising and then the sound of a door closing.

"Storm? Are you safe?" Davy's voice held worry.

"We are now. I just avoided getting run off the road." Storm's eyes were in constant motion.

Teagan stared at him, a frown on her face. Did he really say that, Lord? That we're safe? I wouldn't call this very safe.

"What? They found you?" Davy was troubled, searching through the papers on his desk. "That's what the word has been. That they tracked you somehow. But how?"

"I don't know, Davy. I searched the car before we left. Nothing. The duffle bags? From my house and nothing. My clothes? Nothing. Teagan had all new clothes. Suzy would have checked them before she left them." Storm's teeth pulled at his lip. "I checked my security feed. No one was in or out other than Suzy and us. So, how did they do it?"

"Phones?" Davy was desperate to find out how Storm had been found.

"Turned off. I only turn mine on when I need to call you or Will. Teagan's phone has been off since we retrieved it. Rogan wouldn't have let anyone near it."

"No, he wouldn't. I spoke with him. He's worried, Storm. There has been a man around the mission, looking for you two."

"Par for the course. Listen, Davy, what can you tell me?" Storm studied Teagan, seeing the fear lurking in her eyes.

"Not a lot. We need you two to stay away for now, just as Will said. The group that went in? From what we have been able to determine, they're a nasty bunch, linked to international crime."

"And that means we have to have international forces involved. This just gets better and better. Any more word on why Teagan?"

Davy sighed. Storm had gone to the heart of the issue.

"There is. Apparently, the word that is out there is that she dummied up the reports, making them seem innocent to cover her boss' false reports. Only, that didn't happen. Our IT people have verified the time stamp on her version and what was printed. The reports were dummied up after she had saved the final draft that she was working on. Just why and who? We don't know. And you know that we are investigating all the people involved in that business and then working out from there."

"I know, Davy. It just doesn't make a lot of sense. I had a thought. What happened? That was a cover story to get to Teagan. She's whom they seemed to have wanted. What if it is her and not the company? I'm certain that you are looking into her family and friends." Storm heard the disbelieving cry that Teagan gave and he shook his head at her.

"We are, Storm. I'm on the line of someone, who has gone into hiding. That person may well be one that is behind this. Stay safe. Check in with me late this afternoon. If I need to, I'll leave voice mail." Davy was gone before Storm could respond.

The ringing of his phone startled both of them, and Storm almost dropped his phone. He stared at it and sighed. He needed to talk with his father, only he didn't really want to.

"Dad?"

"Storm?" His father's voice echoed across the airwaves. "Are you okay? You didn't call last night, not like you normally do."

"I know, Dad. I'm in the middle of a situation."

"I gathered that. Head here, Storm. We'll look after this." His father's voice died away as the phone clicked off.

Teagan stared at Storm as he thoughtfully turned off his phone and pocketed it.

—

"Storm? What is that all about?" When he didn't respond, she reached for the door handle, only stopping as his hand grasped her wrist.

"I mean it, Teagan. I will handcuff you to something in this car. You have to stop threatening to run. That will get you killed. Davy let me know that you are the one those men wanted. As to why? He's working on that."

"I get that. But your father? He called you?" Teagan was dumbfounded that he had. It was not what she was used to.

"He did. And we are heading that way." He looked up as he heard a vehicle and sighed. Brownie had just found him.

———

Chapter 11

Teagan shook her head. There was no way this was about her. At least, she didn't think it was. She had been a good girl all her life, she thought, never in trouble, didn't do drugs or alcohol or hang out with the wrong people. So why her?

"I don't get that, Storm. Why me? I didn't do anything."

"We know that, Teagan. It's just that we have to work through everything. Your family. Your friends. Whatever work you did in the past. People that you may know. It takes time."

"And what you're not saying is that I might not have time." Teagan was growing angry. Angry at the situation. Angry at life. Angry at Storm. And even angry at God. He had allowed this, hadn't He? And she just didn't understand why.

Storm shook his head at her even as he stepped from the vehicle. Brownie stared at him for a moment and then ducked his head to stare into the car at Teagan.

"Storm? Just what have you gone and done?"

"Saved a lady from being abducted." Storm leaned against his car, his hands dug into his jeans pockets. "And we don't know why."

"You're a long way from home. Is there a reason?" Brownie leaned back on the car as well.

—

"And are you the one someone complained about on the highway?"

"More than likely. But the only vehicle was the truck that tried to run me off the road. It had to be them that reported me."

"I would imagine it was. Can you explain?"

"Just between you and me. We need it kept quiet. We have a leak somewhere in our department. Will sent me out of town with Teagan, just to keep her safe. Only they've found me."

"And just how did they do that?" Brownie was puzzled, his mind working through the possibilities.

"I have no idea. As far as I know we don't have anything tracking us." He stared at Brownie as the other man suddenly pushed away from the car and walked around to the back.

Brownie paused, his surmise correct.

"A tracking dart, Storm. Somehow they made you and did this." Brownie pointed to the object.

"And I would not have expected that." He reached into his pocket to pull out gloves. Pulling the dart from the car, he turned to Brownie, dropping it into the evidence bag held open for him. "And now what?"

"Now what? You leave town and find somewhere else to go. I'll look after this for you."

A few more words of quiet conversation and Brownie walked back to his car, driving away. Storm slipped back into his and then pulled away, a finger up to stop Teagan's words.

"Storm? What was that all about? And just where are we heading?" Teagan finally spoke, unable to contain her words any longer.

"That? A GPS dart in the back of my car. That's how they found us. And as to where we're heading? To a cottage that my parents have near here. They're likely at it right now. Dad asked me to head that way." He shot her a look as he pulled off onto a gravel road.

"Just like that? We're heading for your parents? I like how you asked me." Teagan turned from him, anger emanating from her, her arms folded across her abdomen.

"Get over your mad, Teagan. This is about keeping you alive until Davy finds out what is going on. And if I have to, I'll take you back to Will and he can lock you up somewhere. Only, you'll not likely survive that seeing how someone is one step ahead of us right now."

"I'm not going there." She refused to look at him, a mutinous look on her face.

"There's no point in pouting, Teagan. It's where we are both heading. Live with it. If you don't, you might not live at all." Storm's attention went back to the traffic around him, finding little in way of that. He sighed. This was not how this week was to have gone, he thought. No, he was to have gone on vacation tomorrow for three weeks. He had had plans to leave town and find somewhere he could hide away from everyone for a few days. Storm was worn out, he knew, and needed that break. Only that break was no longer in the works for him. He was

---

hiding away from everyone, or almost everyone, but that was to keep a beautiful lady alive.

54

Chapter 12

Teagan stared at the cottage that Storm had stopped in front of. *This is it, isn't it, Lord? Is this where I make my stand? Where I live or die? Storm has scared me, and it takes a lot to do that. But why me? I don't get it.*

Storm watched Teagan closely, not sure if he had made the right move coming to his parents' cottage. His father, a minister for a nearby church, stood and watched his son, a frown on his face. His mother stood beside her husband, her hand on his arm.

"What is going on with Storm?" Belle's voice was low, worry evident in it.

"I don't know, Belle. I just know that he needs us and our prayers. We've both been burdened about him the last few days." Philip looked down at his wife for a moment. "And the young lady? He's likely trying his best to keep her alive."

"I am sure that he is. But what if Peter and Paige show up?"

"If they do, they do. Storm will do his utmost to keep his brother and sister alive. You know that." Philip moved away from his wife, to stand near his son's car.

Storm stared at his father for a moment before he was out of the car, greeting him.

—

"Son?   What have you gone and done?" Thurlow's head dipped as he watched Teagan closely.

"Just doing my job, Dad.   Trying to keep someone alive." Storm sighed, weary beyond what he had experienced in a while.   "That's Teagan. Someone is searching for her. The office where she worked? Everyone else killed."

"That's not good, son. Bring her in. It's almost lunchtime and I know your mom has something ready for us."

Storm nodded as he rounded the car, the door open, and his hand drawing Teagan from her seat.

"Teagan, this is my dad, Philip. That's my mom, Isabelle, or Belle as Dad calls her. You're welcome in their home." He watched her closely, knowing that she would just turn and run back down the road if he let her have even a moment on her own. "And don't run. I will handcuff you to something if you even think about it."

Teagan greeted him and then moved past the two men, heading towards Belle, who simply hugged the younger woman before moving them into the house.

"She's hurting, son."

"She is, Dad. She can't see her brother and sister. Her home was burnt down. She was abducted, got away, and then has had to hide. She's also struggling with how God is allowing all this."

"I can see that." Philip's arm was around his son.   His worry over the past few days had intensified. He would do what he could to help. But it was ultimately in God's hands what happened or what He allowed. He firmly believed that and he knew that Storm did as well.

"Thanks, Dad. She's trying her best to run. And I can't have her doing that. I'll have to go after her if she does." Storm stood watching the cottage, a troubled look on his face.

His father, watching closely, saw a look in his son's eyes. A look that he and Belle had waited for years to see. He sighed to himself. He's gone and done it, hasn't he, Lord? Found his lady, while she is in danger and he's trying to protect her, just like his friends. How do we now do this?

"Dad? Your internet is working?"

Philip was not surprised at Storm's question. He knew Storm would be working to figure it all out, as Belle would have said.

"It is, son. But there's another problem. You have never brought a young lady here, not in your entire life. How do you explain that? You can't say that you're protecting her. That would lead them right to you."

"I know, Dad." Storm gave a huge groan. His father had reached right to the centre of his current problem. "I can't say why she's here. But I also can't lie."

"We'll figure it out. Come on, son. We'll eat. Then, I want to spend some time in the Scriptures with both of you and pray for you. Is she a Christian?"

Storm hesitated and then nodded.

"She is, Dad, from what little she has said. But she has to be hurting right now. It's hard on her to be on the run. I don't like doing this, us single people. It's not me to be travelling around with her on my own."

"No, it's not, Storm. That's something else we will have to discuss. And you need to call whoever it is that you are in touch with. There's something going on there that you're not saying." His hand went up as Storm opened his mouth. "You wouldn't be out here as you are if it was safe back there."

Chapter 13

Finding her way to the dock area, Teagan stood for a moment, her eyes on the lake before they rose to the other side of the lake. She could feel peace here, peace that she had been looking for and that she had been for quite a while, she decided. *God, are You there? Will You protect me? Philip brought up so many verses for protection and safety. I know that I have read them, memorized some, and needed that reminder.*

Storm watched her closely before he moved towards her, to come to a stop beside her. An arm came to hug her. Teagan tensed for a moment and then leaned against him. Without realizing it, she was falling in love with Storm. Part of how she was acting was fear for him and what the men would do to her.

"Storm? Where do we go from here? We can't stay here forever."

Storm sighed. Teagan had gotten right to the point, which he had expected her to do.

"For now, we can. It's just how we describe you to the town. That's the problem. I've never brought any lady here, not on her own. Not in my entire life."

Teagan drew a deep breath. This is where I need to leave, she thought. I need to leave and find some way to stay safe.

—

"And no, you're not leaving. You're still in my protective custody. Only we can't tell the town that. But they will try and keep you safe. That goes without saying. Just because of Mom and Dad."

"They will? They can't do that!" Teagan was horrified at the thought.

"They can and will. But how do we explain you away?" He thought through what he needed to say. "I've looked over the paperwork that Will and Brownie have sent me. They're not really much further ahead, although they did find the leak in our department. One of our patrol officers. She's been arrested and is behind bars right now."

"But that still doesn't solve it. I can't figure it out, Storm. Why me?" Teagan stared at the lake. "How deep is the lake?"

Storm shrugged. "Deep. It's friendly today. We can likely go out in the canoes or kayaks if you want to."

Teagan shook her head.

"Not tonight, Storm. I think I need to sleep more than anything else. It's peaceful here, watching the water and the waves."

"It is. When I see the waves and am out on the water, I remember Who it was that calmed the storms. He calms my storms today. Trust Him to do that for you, Teagan." Storm didn't look at her, didn't see her surprised look and then nod of comprehension.

"He does that, doesn't He? We forget. We are so determined to stand on our own two feet and make it through life on our own. It doesn't work out that well."

Storm turned his head, his eyes on her face, seeing the sadness there.

"What happened in your past, Teagan? What destroyed your peace?" He prayed for the lady beside him, knowing that was what he desired for her, for her to find peace once more.

Teagan shook for a moment. No one had ever asked her that in her life. Her peace had been destroyed and she had walked away from her family and her Lord. Even though she still did things with her family, she held back a part of her. Storm was not letting her get away from that. She realized that part of why she was trying too hard to run from him right now was not the threat from the men. It was the burden that she carried, the burden of just what it was now, she couldn't remember.

Shrugging, Teagan just didn't answer. She wasn't ready to bring up the past, to study it, to find out what happened that had destroyed that. She knew that she had to at some time but right now? She was too involved in staying alive, not realizing that God could and would use that very circumstance and situation to bring her back into a closer walk with Him.

"So, Storm, how do we do this? How do we explain me away?" Teagan was tired and combative once more.

"I have no idea, Teagan. We're not getting married, that's a given. The only other way is for us to pretend to be a couple." Storm caught the look on her face. "How else do we explain it?"

Teagan shrugged, turning away from him and heading back inside, to the bedroom that she had been told to consider hers. Storm watched her, before his head dropped. That wasn't what he had wanted to say but it had needed to be said. That he knew. He frowned as he felt his phone vibrating. Davy wanted to talk with him. But did he want to speak with Davy? That was the question.

Chapter 14

"Davy?" Storm sat at his father's desk in his study, a pad of paper and pen at hand. "You needed to speak with me?"

"I did, Storm." Storm could hear Davy shuffling papers. "I'm working at home right now, so we're good to talk. If you are."

"I am. I won't say where I am, though." Storm stared across the room at the shelves filled with his father's books. "We're safe for now, but I can't guarantee for how long. What do you have, Davy?" He waited, not hearing Davy respond. "Davy?"

"Sorry, Storm. Will just got here. He wants to be in on the talk. And Barnabas called. He's worried about you. He wanted you to know that the Foundation is willing to help in any way that they can. Including Andy flying you somewhere."

"Tell him thanks. For now, we're good here. For now anyway. It's just how to explain her to the town." Storm sighed. That had been puzzling him since he had spoken with Teagan the day before.

"I can see that. I have a good idea where you're at right now." Davy shared a look with Will. "Be very careful, the both of you. Don't let her out of your sight."

"I've threatened to handcuff her to me or some inanimate object just to do that. Teagan's ready to

—

run, Davy. And if she does, she disappears." Storm was more worried than he thought he had been.

"She'll try that, Storm." Will spoke up. "If she does, you'll be after her. That puts you in more danger."

"I know, Will. I know that. I just can't get through to her. Did you hear from Brownie?"

"We did. And we found out when it happened. It was as you left the police lot." Davy was frustrated. "We tracked down the youth and it was a youth. He can't tell us much other than he was hired to do that. He was told he wouldn't face charges for that act."

"And he will, considering the circumstances. Is he talking?"

"No, he's not. And he is related to the patrol officer." Will was frustrated, to say the least.

"He is? Her son, I would imagine." Hearing a noise, Storm rose and found Teagan standing just outside of the doorway. His hand reached for hers and pulled her into the room. Shoving her into a chair, he bit back a grin at her glare. "Will, Davy. Teagan has joined us. Maybe you'll be able to explain to her why she needs to stay safe. She's obviously not listening too well to me." He simply stared back at her, his face expressionless, as she glared at him, her mouth open to comment.

"Teagan? We have not spoken, but I am Will Peters, Chief of Police in our town. And Davy Smithson is the detective assigned to your case. First, I know that you are feeling trapped and caged.

—

Unfortunately, there is not a lot that we can do about that, in order to keep you safe."

"Well, I am. I want to go home. Only I don't have a home to go to. And I need to speak with the insurance adjuster, don't I? Just how do I do that?" Teagan went on the offensive, having decided that she would not sit back and wait for whatever it was to come at her.

"We know that, Teagan. We can make arrangements for the adjuster to call you on Storm's phone today. In fact, he asked for that." Davy thought through what needed to be done. "If you need to, fax in authorization for someone to speak with them for you."

"I don't think so. I look after myself, thank you very much." Teagan refused to look at Storm, thinking that she would see horror on his face because of how she was speaking with the police.

Storm simply shook his head, knowing that Teagan was more scared than she wanted to admit.

"Okay, Davy. Where do we stand with the investigation? What can you tell Teagan?" The three men knew there would be details that they could not give her, or could not even give to Storm.

Will and Davy exchanged glances, knowing that they could not talk freely with Storm while Teagan was there. But there was information that they could and would share with her.

"The officer that was hurt? How is he?" Teagan kept her eyes on the floor, certain that she would be blamed for him being wounded.

"Tad? He's recovering, Teagan. We didn't expect it but he is alive, healing, and will come home in the next few days. He has asked about you, wanting to know that you are safe." Will had spoken at length with Tad.

"That's good. I'm glad. I hate that he was hurt because of me. What about my boss? I know Storm said that he was killed. How is his family?" Teagan finally looked up at Storm, finding only concern and compassion on his face. It was the look in his eyes that had her frowning. A look that said that she was special, wanted, loved, and cherished. She frowned at that.

"They're doing as well as they can be right now. They're into counselling, at our request. They are concerned about you. They're working with Davy and the other investigators to help sort through his office. We would have asked that of you, but you can't be here." Will was frustrated, to say the least. "Davy will update you on that as he can. For now, stay where you are. Stay as safe as you can. I know it's not what you wanted to hear, Teagan. It never is. But trust Storm. He has instincts that few officers have, having worked the streets. He's learned what to watch for and how to stay as safe as possible." Will and Davy were gone with that.

Teagan stared at Storm's phone, frustration evident on her face. How do I do that, Lord? How do I stay safe without endangering anyone else? I don't think that's possible. She looked up at Storm, to find him sorting through his notes.

"Storm?"

Her voice saying his name raised his head to watch her before he drew a deep breath. Davy had sent on information to him, information that he needed to work through, and just didn't think that he could at the moment.

"Teagan? For now, we'll set this aside. I have to sort through what I've been sent. I promise. I will tell you what I can. For now, what do you want to do?" He sat back in the chair, his eyes on her, watching closely.

"Me? I have no idea. I don't know what I'm allowed to do." Teagan rose, walking away from him, leaving Storm to rise and follow her to the back yard and then to the dock, standing just behind her, watching the area around her.

Chapter 15

Her hand tight in Storm's, Teagan stared at the main street in the town or village or whatever it was where his parents lived. She wasn't sure at all about being out there, but he had insisted that she needed to. His eyes on her, Storm simply waited for Teagan to move forward, patience learned on the street helping him.

"Teagan? You need stuff, you said. This is one way to get it. You shop for yourself. Mom would have gladly done it, but she doesn't know you or what you like."

"I know, Storm. I just don't feel comfortable doing this. Does that even make sense?"

"It does. Teagan, let's keep moving." Storm's eyes were in constant motion, feeling someone out there. Just who and where, that was what he didn't know.

Teagan finally nodded, walking beside him as he crossed the street, heading for a small cafe.

"Storm? It's early. We haven't even shopped." Teagan protested as he held the door for her.

"I know, but this is the best way to get word out that you are a friend. It will happen whether we want it to or not. This way? We can control to a certain extent what happens. I know it's not keeping you hidden. That's not going to work, no matter what we do. They've proven that they can find you. I would hazard a guess that they know who our families are and have tracked them down."

Teagan stared at him for a moment even as she reached for the menu sitting on the table in the booth that he had chosen. She shook her head. *This is what they meant, isn't it, Lord? That our families will be at risk. How do we trust? How do we find peace in all of this? Storm has, I can tell, given what he's been through and where he's lived.*

Storm rose at last, reaching for her hand. He decided he liked how it fit with his, only he shouldn't be holding it, he realized. How did he do this, Lord? How did he keep her safe? He knew that she was fast turning into a friend, a feisty one at that, one who kept challenging him.

The townspeople watched Storm and Teagan and then turned to watch the two men or youths who were following them. They stepped in to hide the couple as best they could, hindering the movements of the two following them. That frustrated the followers, who soon lost sight of the couple.

Storm looked around as they walked back to his car, nodding at the townspeople, not knowing for certain but sure that they had stepped in to protect them. It's what he expected of his town. His father was the beloved pastor at a local church. That worked to their advantage. But Storm himself was always ready to lend a hand where needed when he was in town. That endeared him to the townspeople on his own merit.

Teagan searched the area, feeling unsafe. Someone was out there, she was sure, someone who wanted her and wanted her dead. Only she couldn't see them. Not that she would have known them, she thought to herself. Everyone here other than Storm was a stranger to her. She had heard the comments directed at Storm and his laughing deflection of them. *Storm, what did you do? Couldn't you have just said that I was a friend and only here for a short time? But he hadn't. He had not denied any interest in her and that puzzled her.*

Storm headed back towards his parents' home and then pulled off into a picnic area. He was unsure at that point just where to go. He had felt the eyes, the presence of evil that morning as he and Teagan had wandered that town. Storm was hesitant to go near his parents, not wanting to bring any danger to them. Somehow, one of the men had found his cell number. Just how that was, Storm would be looking into. His was an unpublished number and not out there for public view. He suspected the officer that had been arrested. She would have had access to his number and passed it on. The threat towards himself and Teagan had been forwarded to Davy. Storm had not heard back from him as yet.

"Storm? Aren't we going to your parents? Or have you decided that you just want to stop in random spots and not move at all?" Teagan was puzzled and it came out in her words.

"Enough, Teagan. We were followed today. And somehow someone has my cell number. It should be out there and it is."

—

"How can that be?" Teagan stared at him before looking out of the side window.

"Someone, likely the officer arrested, had access to it. I will not show you the message. It was nasty. They are looking for you, know that you are with me, and state that they are coming for you." Storm's phone was out and he checked his messages, sighing to himself as he saw Davy's response. It had been what he had expected it to be. "I sent it on to Davy. He'll work it."

"He can't. He has other cases to work."

"No, he's working ours. It's just not that three people were murdered. It's that a police officer was injured. Another police officer is on the run and in hiding. There is a witness whose life is at stake. What more can I tell you?" Storm's words came out in a biting manner, causing Teagan to jump and turn and stare at him. "We're in danger, Teagan, whether you admit it or not. That's life for us at the present. And it involves our families now, both yours and mine. Will has people with yours. My brother and sister likely have as well. Only, we don't know who is out there, who else has been hired, and just who is it that is behind this all. Isn't that enough?"

Teagan blinked at the rapid words that Storm was shooting at her. She had thought of her own family but not his. Of course, his would be at risk, if they knew who they were.

"How would they know who your family is?"

"That officer? She likely told them. It's easy enough to for her to have found out. And I brought you to Mom and Dad. Now, you tell me. How do we

—

do this? How do we keep you safe and them safe as well? It's not like we're in some movie and we can solve the crime in the next five minutes. It doesn't work that way in real life. Davy has to investigate. Anything he finds has to be proven and documented. He needs that for court. And that's not easy for him right now. He's trying to trace contacts, your family, my family, where you worked before, the business owner, his family and their contacts. Any word from the street he gets? Got it! It has to be investigated and proven. It sometimes takes weeks or months to build a case." Storm was beyond frustrated at this point and yes, he was scared for his family. He just didn't know how they would do this, work through what needed to be done and yet keep everyone safe. It was a given, he thought, that at some point Teagan and he would be found. That danger was a constant source of worry for him.

Teagan stared at him before her anger flared and then did. He's right, isn't he, Lord? How do we do this?

"Can we look into things, Storm? I can't just sit by and let life happen. I need to be involved."

"We can, but I'm not sure where we'll be safe enough to do that." Storm sighed, reaching to start his vehicle and pull away from the picnic area. Only, he never made it out of the area. Teagan's scream was the last thing that he heard. That was, other than the horrible screech and crunch of metal as his car was broadsided and shoved off the road, into a strand of trees, before the truck backed away and disappeared in a cloud of dust and dirt. Teagan's body lay against the door and window, motionless.

—

Storm's body was draped across the steering wheel, the deflated airbags eerily floating around them until they dropped to lay across the dashboard.

73

Chapter 16

Philip turned from the window that he had been staring out of it. It was late afternoon by this time. Storm and Teagan should have been back and weren't. That worried him. In fact, it scared him. Belle walked towards him and into his hug.

"Philip? Where are they? Storm expected to be back by early afternoon at the latest."

"I know, Belle." He turned her towards his study. "I'm reaching out to Chad. He'll send an officer out to patrol the road here."

Belle nodded before she was away, her keys in her hand, stopping as she walked towards her vehicle. She frowned. No, she thought, she didn't know the man walking towards her. An officer, she decided.

"Mrs. Brophy?" The man stopped before he reached her, a hand into his jacket pocket to pull out his identification. "I'm Davy Smithson. I'm looking for Storm."

Belle reached carefully for the wallet, staring at the picture and then the man in front of her before handing it back.

"Storm? Come in. Maybe you can help." Belle led the way back in, finding Philip looking for her. "Philip, this is that Davy whom Storm mentioned. He's looking for Storm."

———

Philip studied the younger man before he nodded.

"That's a problem, Officer. Storm is not here, nor is Teagan. They went into our town this morning and have not yet returned. They should have been back by now and aren't."

Davy's hand froze as he tucked away his identification. This was what he didn't want to hear, but what he had expected to hear at some point.

"Which way to your town?" He spun on his heel, his hand reaching for Philip's arm. "You stay here, Mrs. Brophy." His command had Belle stopping in her tracks

Sliding into his vehicle, Davy sped away, slowing as he reached the highway.

"There is only one way in from here?" He turned his head towards Philip. "Mr. Brophy?"

"It's Philip, please. Yes, unless you take a detour. And Storm wouldn't have done that, not unless he had to." Philip's eyes were moving constantly, watching as a patrol vehicle passed them and then turned to speed around them. "That's Chad, our police chief. Where's he heading? I had just spoken to him before you appeared."

"I see." Davy slowed as the traffic in front of him slowed. He gave an exclamation and then pulled off to the side, his hazard lights on. "Stay here, Philip. I need to see what's going on."

Davy was out of his vehicle, running across the road to the man who Philip had identified as Chad, his identification in his hand.

Chad turned, his keen eyes focused on Davy for a moment.

"And you would be?"

"I'm Davy Smithson, a detective that's been working on Teagan's case. I was sent up here to speak with both Storm and Teagan. Only Philip said they hadn't arrived home yet."

Chat Wells sighed. This was not what he needed, another police force involved in this accident.

"They won't. Somehow or other, Storm's vehicle was broadsided." He nodded towards the strand of trees. "It's in there."

"Storm? Teagan?" Davy shot a look behind him at his vehicle.

"They're inside. The firefighters are working to free them. Philip doesn't need to see this." Chad was a good friend of his pastor, spending a lot of time with him not just for counselling but for Bible study and prayer.

"No, he doesn't, but if he's like his son, he can handle it." Davy waited as Chad stepped away to speak with an officer.

Chad returned, a shadow in his eyes.

"They're alive, Davy. I have no idea how hurt they are. I haven't that information. We'll take them to our hospital. If I could impose on you, could you bring both Philip and Belle to the hospital? I'll speak with Philip."

Chad and Davy walked back towards where Philip waited at the side of the road, somber looks on

—

their faces. Philip took one look at them, fear for his son in his heart. Please, Lord? Let him be alive.

"Philip? I'm sending Davy back to your place to get Belle. He'll stay with you, at my request, and bring you to the hospital." Chad watched with concern as Philip's eyes slid shut. "Philip?"

"Is he alive? That's all I need to know." Philip sought reassurance of that fact from his friend.

"He is. How badly hurt he is or Teagan is? That I don't know. They're working on them. Storm was run off the road sometime this afternoon." Chad's hand went out to grasp Philip's arm, holding him upright. "Let Davy go get Belle and then get you to the hospital. I'll know more by the time that you get there."

Davy and Chad shared a look, knowing that it could still go south, as they phrased it, for either Storm or Teagan or both of them. Philip nodded soberly before he was back in Davy's vehicle, fearing for his son and the young lady that they had welcomed into their home and yes, into their hearts. Both he and Belle had seen the interest in one another that the younger couple was trying hard to hide from one another. He sighed before he began to pray, begging God for the life of his son and the young lady.

Belle stared at Davy for a moment before she reached for a jacket and then her purse, locking the doors behind her and heading for his vehicle. Philip stood waiting for her, simply wrapping her into his arms, a prayer raising for her and their son and their other children, Teagan included in it.

—

Davy watched, sorrow on his face. He had taken an opportunity to send a text off to Will, who had responded with shock and then ordered Davy to stay put. He wanted an update as soon as Davy could provide one.

Chapter 17

Philip paced the waiting room of the local hospital Emergency Department. Belle he knew was seated nearby. Peter and Paige had appeared, having planned on being at their parents' that day, bewildered as to what had happened. Belle had gently explained, an arm around each of her children, her eyes on the doors to the examination rooms.

Davy stood, back to the wall, and watched the four. He was puzzled. He thought that Storm would be safe, even though the word on the street that had reached him was that Storm had been found. Will had called him, anxious for any word. They both felt guilty, even though the decision had been made with the best information that they had at the time.

Chad hesitated as he approached through the doors, stopping by Davy.

"Any word yet?" His voice was low and contained the worry that he was trying hard to hide. He had watched Storm grow from a baby to the young man of today. He had counselled Storm when he had approached him about joining a police force, watching with both interest and concern as Storm had worked his way through the ranks. Those two had had many a conversation over the years on the dangers they both faced.

"Not yet. A nurse was out a bit ago and spoke with Philip. I talked to him after. He said they were working on the two. And could I contact Teagan's family for him?"

"There's that, isn't there? How do we do that? I spoke with your chief. He informed me that he has her parents and siblings tucked away."

"He does, but he'll get them here. I know him that well. He won't keep them apart. I expect that he'll fly them in. Andy from the Barnabas Foundation would have been contacted to do that."

"He would? I've heard good things about the Foundation." Chad watched as a physician emerged, searched and then headed for Davy. "That's John Forbes. He's a deacon at our church. Looks as if he's heading for you."

"So it does." Davy moved away from the wall and approached the physician.

"Dr. Forbes? I'm Detective Davy Smithson. You're wanting to speak with me?"

John nodded, his eyes on Davy and then on Storm's family as they watched.

"I do. I've spoken with Teagan's father, who is her power of attorney. I guess it was your chief who connected us. He gave me permission to speak with you, even though it's not needed." He pointed to the outdoors. "Let's walk. That way we can speak without being overheard." He led the way through the doors, his long white lab coat moving in the breeze that had come up.

"Doctor? What can you tell me?" Davy finally spoke, watching John Forbes closely.

"Teagan's a lucky lady, Detective. Or rather, I should say that God had His hand on her. She's unconscious right now. The airbags did go off, causing some burns to her face, which will heal. She's in imaging right now, just to assess if there are broken bones. Her arm for one is broken. Her hip and leg? Her ribs? That's what we need to assess. She will be heading for surgery to set the arm and shoulder as there seems to be damage to it as well."

Davy winced, thinking of how that would hurt over the next few days.

"Okay. Soft tissue? Internal injuries?"

"That's what we looking at as well. Soft tissue injuries for sure." John shared a look with Chad before he looked at Davy. "Find who did this. She won't survive the next time. This was a deliberate attempt to kill her. You know why, I suspect. Find them and bring them to justice." He turned and walked back into the hospital, leaving Davy staring down at the lines on the pavement.

Chad waited, knowing that Davy had to process the report. Davy finally raised his eyes, blinking for a moment as he sought to control his emotions. Teagan had gone through too much already, he thought, and now this. And he knew that Storm would blame himself for not seeing the truck. Only from what he had been told, they didn't have a chance to avoid it.

"Davy? Your chief has been in touch again. He said that Andy, I think it was, would be landing in the next ten minutes. I have sent patrol vehicles to meet the plane and bring Teagan's family here. But

—

81

we need to talk about this. We need to keep the families safe, to say nothing of Storm and Teagan."

"I know, Chad. Just how do we do that? Your officers can for a while, but not for long term."

"I know. We may need to reach out to a security team to do that." Chad drew a frustrated breath, pulling out his phone and frowning. "Your chief again. He says that he has found a security team and is sending them our way."

"He has?" Davy reached for his own phone and then grinned. "Good. It's Abe Finlay and his team. That means Emma has gotten involved."

"Emma? Who is she?" Chad frowned at Davy as Davy grinned at him.

"Not for common knowledge, but if you have heard of Trackers, then you have heard of Emma. She finds people and information no one else is able to. If she's involved now, and I am sure that she is, she'll be sending us lots of information."

"I've heard of Trackers. In fact, we have that company as consultants, but I'm not sure how she can help in this." Chad moved out of the way as an ambulance approached.

"She will help. In fact, she'll make it a priority for now, unless she gets called into something else. Will said Abe and his team will be here this evening and can stay for a week. We'll reassess after that."

"That we will." Chad pointed to the doors. "In we go. I want to find out if they've been out about Storm."

"I'm sure that they have been. Let's see what was said."

Chapter 18

Philip stared down at his son as he stood beside his stretcher. Belle's arm was around her two other children. Peter and Paige stared down at their brother, not understanding completely what had happened. Storm was still unconscious. That concerned the physician treating him. David Leigh looked up at the family, drawing in a deep breath. *This is never easy, is it, Lord? To have to talk to family members and having to talk to friends.*

"David? What can you tell us?" Philip looked up at David, a frown on his face, worry as well.

"He's still unconscious, as you can see. Brushing for sure. Burns from the airbags. What other damage from them we will have to assess once we can. His left shoulder is damaged. Broken with ligament tears. That we can repair. So far, no internal injuries. His right hand has been broken. How that happened? Likely from him reaching for Teagan, is it?" At Philip's nod, David shifted to look at Belle and then Peter and Paige. He walked away at last, leaving the surgeon to speak with them. He had other patients that he needed to attend to.

Belle watched him walk away before her attention went back to Storm. I

"Philip, have you heard how Teagan is?"

Philip shook his head.

———

"I haven't. They were waiting for her family to come. I think they are likely here now." He moved his family back to the waiting room, knowing that Storm would be going up to surgery soon. He frowned for a moment as he saw a couple around their age with a young man and woman standing, in shock, he thought. "That must be her parents."

Davy had approached the couple, his identification out.

"You're Teagan's folks?"

Teagan's father turned, a frown on his face until he saw Davy's identification.

"We are. We were told that the physician would be out to speak with us but that was thirty minutes ago. We don't know where our daughter is or her condition." To say that Tully Connell was upset would have been an understatement.

"I see. Let's move you four over here. Please, sit. I'll be right back." Davy walked away, the protest on Tully's lips stilling.

"Dad? What is going on? Why is she here?" Tara watched Davy disappear behind the doors, before she shared a look with her brother, Thurlow.

"She was here with the officer providing protection for her. We talked about that last night." Tully knew that Tara would have difficulty accepting that. It was how she was, he thought.

Teagan's mother, Amy, simply shook her head at her daughter.

"You know that, Tara. We've been under protection as well. Now, we wait for the physician to

—

85

appear and then we go see how she is." Amy sat back, her eyes on Philip as he approached.

"Mr. Connell?" Philip's quiet voice had Tully spinning. "I'm Storm's father, Philip Brophy. I'm sorry that we had to meet under these circumstances."

Tully nodded, introducing his family.

"Your son? How is he?"

"He's heading for surgery to repair some broken bones. Other than that, he's in remarkably good shape, all things considered. God had His hand on our family today."

"That he did." Amy had stood, her arm around Tully. "One of the patrol officers said that you were a minister."

"I am. This shows you that bad things can happen to Christians as well as non-Christians. Listen. I have taken the liberty of speaking with one of our church members. They have a cottage on their property, just a couple of blocks from here in fact, that you are welcome to use. The officers know it well."

"Thank you." Tully and Amy were surprised at that. "We expected to find a motel or something like that."

"Not necessary. It's what we do. I know that Jim or Betty will be around to find you at some point over the evening. None of us will be leaving here until we see our kids again. Come, sit with my family. We're united in this, whether that was what we wanted or not. Storm has done best to protect Teagan."

"And she will have protested and tried to run." Tara shrugged at the look thrown at her. "It's what she does."

Chapter 19

Storm moved restlessly on his hospital bed, pain driving him awake. He cracked open his eyes, finding the lighting low and the blinds closed against the night sky. He sighed to himself. *What did I do, Lord?* Shooting to a sitting position, Storm frantically searched the room. *No, Teagan was not there. Just where was she?*

He was on his feet, ignoring the cold floor and the pain from his shoulder at his sudden movements. He searched for his clothes, dressing as rapidly as he could. Storm stared at his shirt, knowing that he couldn't put it on.

Storm headed for the door, opening it and looking around the hallway. Teagan had to be here somewhere, he thought. He walked out, pausing his forward steps as a man around his own age stepped into his line of sight. He remained quiet, waiting for the other man to speak.

Nathaniel, one of Abe's team members, grinned for a moment before he pointed at the room that Storm had just walked out of.

"I don't think that you're supposed to be up and on your feet. I'm Nathaniel, a friend who is here to provide security for you." Nathaniel waited, pulling out his wallet and handing it to Storm.

Storm searched Nathaniel's face and then his identification.

———

"One of Abe's men? I see. Someone called you in."

"Your police chief did. Will spoke with Abe and we headed up here. We're here for a week." Nathaniel pointed behind Storm. "That way, I think, is how you want to proceed. Teagan's in a room just down the hall there. Luke is on duty with her."

"He is? How many are there of you?" Storm walked carefully that way, his head pounding. He knew that he shouldn't be up, but duty and something else was driving him to find Teagan. She had become his lady, only he didn't want to acknowledge that. Not yet, anyway.

Hesitating for a moment before he shoved the door open, Storm's thoughts turned to Teagan even as he began to pray for her. *She's feisty, Lord, but that's what will keep her alive. As long as I can keep her from running, that is. And that's a real danger. She'll take off, without me knowing, and I won't find her in time.* He frowned, bringing Luke's and Nathaniel's eyes to his face. *How did they find us like that, Lord? I was watching. I was careful. But it wasn't enough. I need to talk to Davy, only he's not here.*

Walking towards the bed, Storm prayed as he had never prayed before. He didn't know the extent of Teagan's injuries and was afraid for her. He breathed a sigh of relief as he studied her. Shoulder and arm, bruising, burns from the airbags. But there could be residual damage from those airbags. And that frightened him.

He watched her face closely, seeing the movements that said she was beginning to rouse. *How long will you need to be in here, Teagan? And where do we take you to heal? Not back to Mom and Dad's. Not to your parents.* A thought stopped him. *Had anyone contacted her family? That he would have to ask.*

Storm's hand settled on Teagan's free hand, stilling her movement. He prayed, asking for peace in the situation for them both, even as Teagan's eyes opened and she looked around, fear on her face until her eyes focused on him.

"Hi!" Her voice was rough with pain. "What happened?"

"We were hit and ended up here. Has anyone been around to talk to you?"

"There was. A surgeon, I think. He said I broke my arm and damaged ligaments or tendons or something in my shoulder. Bruising. He's wanting to assess me for other damage. That I don't understand."

"The airbags went off. And that can cause damage that we don't know about. Did they say when you could leave?"

"This morning, as long as I had someone to help me. Only I don't. I know my parents and siblings are here. Mom was in really late and talked to me. Will, I guess, made arrangements for them to be flown in. They're staying for a few days, I think, or maybe I just heard wrong."

"They will be." A man's voice that they didn't recognize had both Storm and Teagan jumping. "I'm

---

Abe Finlay. My team's with you for the next week. But don't be surprised if we move you in the middle of the night. That may happen." Abe studied them even as he grinned. "Andy brought your family in, Teagan. They stay until late this evening and he flies them back to your town and protection once more. Your sister's complaining."

"Tara will. She makes noise just for the sake of making noise. She always has." Teagan rested her head back on the pillow, not realizing that Storm still held her hand.

Abe studied the two and nodded to himself. *A couple,* he thought, *just like my team and so many of our friends and acquaintances.*

"My wife, Emma, is researching the names she has been provided. Any information goes to Davy. Now about where you two will go?" Abe pointed towards the door. "Storm, you were not to be up and on your feet. Not yet."

"I know, but I had to. It's not the first time I've been injured."

"No, it's not. But it's different this time. This was a directed hit at you, aiming to take you out so that they could get to Teagan. Something scared them off and I for one would like to know why. Davy's spoken with me. There is a hit out on you. And by hit, I mean your death simply because you stepped in as the officer protecting Teagan. It doesn't matter who it was. Any officer in your boots would have been targeted. Our duty is to keep you safe for the next few days before we take you somewhere."

—

"I'm not going anywhere else." Teagan's mutinous look had no effect on Abe.

"Doesn't matter, Teagan. You don't have a choice. If you don't, you'll disappear. Others may be hurt or killed just because they get in the way. Can you live with that?" Abe's words sounded brutal but he knew from experience that he had to be with Teagan. She wouldn't listen any other way.

Chapter 20

Storm wandered his parents' home later that afternoon. The surgeon had agreed to release them with the condition that they go somewhere that they would be looked after. That was not on their own, he stressed. They would be hurting soon and badly.

Teagan had not responded to that, simply taking her discharge papers and waiting for Abe's men to move them away from the hospital. Her family had spent much of the day with her before Andy flew out with them, heading home. Storm, she knew, wanted to talk with her but she just kept walking away from him. Storm allowed that for now but he knew it would have to change.

Abe stared between the two. He had talked at length with Davy, Chad, and then Will. He was moving them, back to their home town, but not to a home. Barnabas had been in touch, offering suites in the Foundation building. Abe knew the building, knew that they had security on site all the time, and that an Emergency Room physician and his wife, a retired nurse, were on site, as well as the building having an on-site infirmary. It was the best place for them, he agreed, for now. If it came to it, he would take them back to his home and set them up in cabins in the village that had developed from his compound. He had a paramedic on his team who would gladly watch over them.

—

Storm sighed to himself even as he sat, a hand resting on the sling he was wearing. He could hear his parents talking in the kitchen. His brother and sister had had to head home, work duties calling them back. He was frustrated to say the least and worried. *How was he to keep Teagan safe now? Lord, please? I need to protect this lady and can't. The surgeon said four weeks in the cast and then physiotherapy. That means weeks I am off. I can no longer be the officer protecting her. But who do we bring in? Will hasn't said, not yet.*

Abe sat across from Storm, his gaze shifting between Teagan and Storm. This is where it always gets difficult, he thought. He prayed even as he watched the two.

"Storm, Teagan? We need to talk. Teagan, you need to sit and sit now." Abe was stern, but knew he had to be. He watched with some amusement as Teagan finally sat, a blank look on her face as she stared at him. "We're keeping you two here until tomorrow. Then, we move you. No, we won't say until we're on the road. And it means that you two travel separately."

Storm nodded, knowing that ha to be the case. He watched Teagan, seeing her trying to understand what Abe meant.

"Abe means that if we travel separately, we have a better chance of survival. He will have four of his men with each of us. And before you ask, Abe's team is highly skilled and trained. This is what they do, Teagan. Provide security."

Teagan finally nodded. "Where?"

"That we will tell you once we're on the road. It's safest that way. For the rest of today and tonight, relax as much as you can. Get some sleep. We'll likely be on the road very early in the morning. Before it gets light."

He grinned as Teagan snorted.

"That's about what I thought you would say. Storm, we never did get out in the canoe."

"No, we didn't. We'll have other chances to do that, once this threat is behind you."

Storm's words brought Teagan's eyes to his, a frown on her face. *What does he mean, Lord? Once this is over, we walk away from one another. Maybe pass each other at church or in town. But our friendship will be over, won't it?*

Storm's eyes closed as he drifted off, the pain medications kicking in. Abe was on his feet, heading for his business partner, Murphy, to go over plans for the morning. Teagan was at a loss, not wanting to leave Storm but not wanting to stay. Belle watched for a moment before she was drawing Teagan to her feet and to the room that she had been using. She watched closely as Teagan finally laid down and then drew a blanket over her. Belle's hand rested on Teagan's head as she prayed for her. Teagan had become important to them, firstly because they could see that she had become important to Storm, but secondly because she had become dear to them all on her own.

Chad turned from the back door as Belle entered the kitchen, his eyes kindly. He knew that Belle and Philip were deeply worried about their son

—

and his lady, as Belle had taken to calling Teagan. The next few days and weeks would be difficult for both families, that much he knew. He had talked in depth with Will, Davy, and Abe, knowing that they were all involved in protecting these two young people, but not quite sure how to do just that.

Chapter 21

Teagan stared out the window of the SUV, looking past Joseph who sat beside her, his eyes occasionally watching her. She was frustrated, hurting, and just wanting this over. Only it didn't seem that would be the case. Abe was in the front passenger seat, his business partner with Storm. Storm had wanted to talk last night. Only she hadn't wanted that and walked away from him.

Abe watched closely, through the brightening of the dawn sky. So far, he thought, they were safe but that could change in an instant. He knew that Teagan was ready to run. And if she did, they couldn't stop her. Only, Storm would go after her, leaving both of them at the mercy of whoever it was that wanted them dead. And that had become very clear. That was exactly what was wanted. It was only God's protection, he acknowledged, that had saved their lives two days before.

Watching as Luke pulled to a stop in a parking lot in their town, Teagan sighed. Back home again, back where it all started. Now what?

Abe was out of the SUV heading for Murphy who walked towards him. Joseph, Luke, and Matt stepped from the vehicle, their eyes searching for anything that was off. Teagan watched and then took advantage of an open door and a moment when the men were not watching her. She slipped away,

—

heading for the trees on the edge of the lot, disappearing from view. Joseph stared in disbelief into the empty vehicle before the three men were searching.

Storm stood and watched, shaking his head. Of course, she would do this. It was par for the course of what was happening. But where would she go? To her parents? That he really didn't know.

Murphy stood beside him, his gaze shifting between Storm and Abe.

"Did you know that she'd do this?"

Storm shrugged, not willing to commit.

"I had an idea that she would try something, just not this soon." Storm sighed. "Just take me to my home, Murphy. There's no point in heading for the Foundation building. Teagan was who we were trying to keep safe."

"They'll go after you." Abe walked up to him, frustration evident.

"No, they won't. They know she's not with me. They'll look for her. I'll put out word on the streets. My friends will watch out for her."

Storm wandered his home late that night, a mug of coffee in his hand before he stood at the front door, his hand resting against the glass as he stared out into the night. *Just where are you, Teagan? Your mom called looking for you. You weren't there. Your home is not there for you. Where would you go to? Lord, please? Keep my lady safe. Bring her back to us.* Storm was not aware that his thoughts regarding Teagan had changed that much, that he thought of her

---

98

as his lady now, not just as someone he was directed to keep safe.

A week went by and then another one. Davy had been around, assessing Storm, questioning if he knew where Teagan was. All Storm could do was shake his head. He had no idea where she was. He had searched, had spoken with her family, to no avail. His shoulder had healed enough that he could go without the sling. Storm was glad for that but frustrated that he still could not use it as well as he had once. Physiotherapy was happening but it would take time, he was told.

Over the two weeks, Teagan watched Storm from the shadows as she put it. She didn't want harm to come to him, but she couldn't be in touch with him. She felt it too dangerous. Only Teagan didn't know the danger that lay in wait for her. She knew that she needed to find somewhere to stay. Her home wasn't an option not until it was repaired. She refused to go to her family. That would put them at too much risk. Teagan signed to herself. That left only one option. The streets. She just wasn't sure if that was the right move.

Turning and trudging away from where she had stood, watching Storm as he searched for her, she looked for a building where she could stay, out of the cold and wet. She didn't hear the footsteps rapidly approaching her until her wrist was grasped in a hard grip and she was pulled away from the building that she had just decided would work for the night. She struggled to get away, without any success.

She was shoved into an empty building, her fear taking away her ability to think or plan or even try to escape. The man who had captured her simply moved her to a corner and then stood in front of her, back to her, watching the door. He felt that they had been seen. The man, Angus by name, had been watching her. Not for the man who headed the gang that had been involved in the shooting at her work place. This was personal for him. He was after Storm and thought that taking his lady would bring him out.

Angus grasped her wrist once more in a tight, hurting grip and pulled her with him, shoving her into another building and into a room. The door was slammed and a padlock fastened through the shiny new hasp on the door. He gave an evil grin. Angus was ecstatic. He had possession, as he termed it, of Storm's woman. She wouldn't be going back to him, not yet. Or perhaps never.

Teagan picked herself up from the cold, dirty, garbage-strewn floor and flew to the door. She banged on it and yelled and pulled at the door, unable to budge it. No one answered her calls for help. She turned, looking around the dusky, poorly-lit room, finding not much there. A rough pile of blankets were in a corner. A dirty, ragged, and torn curtain hid the crude amenities.

She sank down on the floor, her head buried in her arms. Who had taken her, she wondered? And why? The man had not said anything at all as to why, just gloated almost as he watched her. He was unkempt, his clothing dirty and rough. A ragged beard covered his face and his hair was uncut. She could smell the alcohol and tobacco on him and that turned her stomach. Teagan couldn't pray. She didn't think God would hear her any more, at least, that's what she thought. How she was to get away, she had no idea. She only begged that Storm be kept safe.

Chapter 22

Two weeks passed for Teagan. She was kept locked in that room, provided with little in the way of food. Water was given to her but nothing else to drink. She felt filthy and ashamed of herself.

Angus appeared multiple times in a day, at first just to stand in front of her. If she looked at him, she was slapped and beaten. The daily abuse had begun to take its toll on her. Teagan was losing herself in the shame of the abuse, beaten down until she no longer yelled at him or asked to be released. She just didn't speak.

His words beat at her spirit, his words that she was no good, that she was useless and worthless. She had begun to believe the words spit at her in anger every day.

Then, the day came that he began to parade her through the streets, her wrist in his tight, hard, hurting grasp. She refused to look up, even though Storm's friends watched her. They were willing to help her, if only she had asked. Teagan had come to the point that she had just given up.

Angus pulled her with him towards a home one day, her feet reluctant to move, Storm's home, in fact. He wanted Storm to see that he had Storm's lady and that he was the victor. Just why that was? Teagan didn't know and really wasn't sure that she wanted to.

Her prayers, she felt, reached nowhere even though they were heard.

Angus pulled Teagan past Storm's house, not knowing or caring if he was seen. In fact, that was exactly what he wanted. He wanted Storm to come out and challenge him. Only, Storm didn't appear. Storm was in the downtown area, working another case.

Old Bill watched Storm closely before he took a moment to approach his friend. Storm stood, his notebook on the hood of his car as he made notes. His thoughts were on the scuffle or trouble or whatever you wanted to call it that he had been called in on. Teenagers fighting with teenagers. Only this time weapons had been involved and multiple teens injured.

"Storm?" Old Bill's voice brought Storm's head up as he looked around. "We need to talk."

"We do? Can you give me about five minutes, just to finish my notes?" Storm was torn, knowing that Old Bill would not have approached him when he was working unless he had good reason to.

Old Bill stepped back into the shadows of the buildings, knowing that Storm would find him.

Storm stood upright at long last, his eyes on the scene in front of him. A chaotic scene, he thought, of youths that had been involved in a brawl, leaving a number injured. He sighed. Sometimes the cruelty of a young person just drained him. His notebook and pen tucked away, he sighed once more. Old Bill was waiting for him, he knew. His eyes searched, finding a small diner just down the road from where he stood.

He walked towards Old Bill, before pointing towards it.

Old Bill nodded, knowing that Storm needed that time to decompress, to right his spirit somewhat. He had watched the scene from the first moments that it began, wishing it had been different, but knowing that it wouldn't be. He slid onto a bench seat in a booth, looking up to thank the waitress as she filled their coffee cups. She shot them both a smile before she walked away, leaving menus on the table for them.

Storm watched Old Bill, seeing the distress that he was trying hard to hide. He raised his mug of coffee, sipping at it as he waited for his companion to speak.

It was as they were finishing their meal that Old Bill finally looked across the table at him, assessing Storm and nodding. Storm was healing, he thought, at least physically. He was missing Teagan, that much Old Bill knew.

"I've seen Teagan, Storm." His quiet words were almost missed.

Storm nodded, before his head shot up and he stared at Old Bill.

"You've seen her? Is she okay? And where?" Storm kept his voice low, not sure if anyone in the diner would be able to hear him. He had searched daily for Teagan, not finding her. His friends on the streets had told him that they had seen her but only briefly.

"No, Storm. No, she's not. She's being held against her will." Old Bill was sober, almost in tears.

He had connected with Teagan, with her fiery spirit and sass. "I'm trying to find the building where she's at, but I just can't."

"Who has her?" Storm kept his eyes steady on his friend. "Whereabouts in the downtown area?"

"It's not quite in the downtown area, I don't think. His name is Angus. He's known on the streets. A very brutal man. I fear for her." Old Bill's mouth trembled as he remembered seeing her just that morning, pulled along the streets by the monster as he termed him.

"Angus? He has her?" Storm sat back, despair on his face, even as he blew out a breath. His phone vibrated and he pulled it out, paling as he read it. Money dropped on the table for their meal, Storm was on his feet, pulling Old Bill with him.

Old Bill stumbled a bit at first, trying to keep up with Storm. He wasn't as young as he once was and arthritis was catching up with him.

"Storm?" Old Bill's puzzled voice broke through the darkness that Storm had been under.

"We've found him. Someone reported him." Storm was on the radio, asking for backup, before he shoved at Old Bill. "In, Old Bill. You need to come with me. I know where she is. Backup is coming. But I need you there. You're a witness. If he knows that you saw him, your life is forfeit. You know that."

Old Bill sighed, a deep, weary-to-the-bones sigh, and nodded. He knew the reputation of this man. They needed to get Teagan away from him. Only, how could they?

Chapter 23

Watching from the alleyway that he had stopped in, Storm studied the building in front of him. It was an abandoned house, one that he had used himself at some points during his tenure as an undercover officer. He nodded as Davy approached.

"Have you seen him?" Davy's voice was barely audible.

"Just a glimpse. He's in there." Storm's teeth worried at his lips. "I don't like this, Davy. There are a lot of rooms in there where he could hide. If he has Teagan in there, who knows where he has her hidden."

"She's in there, Storm. I have confirmation of that. Officers are working their way around the house, moving in as close as they can." Davy looked around. "Let's pray and then we'll move in."

Storm moved quickly towards the decrepit front door, Davy behind him. He could hear the footsteps of other officers. He hit the door with his shoulder, the door flying back to bang against the wall that had been damaged by just such moves in the past.

He searched, his weapon in both hands, pointing downwards. The sudden appearance of a large shape in front of him brought him to a sliding halt. Storm's eyes were on Angus before he looked past him. Teagan was there, huddled against a wall, not looking up at all. She doesn't even seem to be aware of her surroundings, Storm thought.

"On your knees! You're under arrest!" Storm's voice was one of many that called out to Angus, who just stood, a smirk on his face.

"Not happening, copper. We're leaving. Me and my women." Angus turned, reaching for Teagan, who shrank back from him.

Storm nodded as a patrol officer simply approached Teagan, wrapping an arm around her and pulling her from the room. He frowned at the lack of resistance that Teagan showed.

Davy was gone, heading for the outside and Teagan. He tucked her into the backseat of a patrol vehicle before he stared back at the house. Once he was seated in the front of the vehicle, the officer drove away, heading for the hospital and safety for Teagan.

Storm approached the man, his weapon now holstered, knowing that he had officers around him ready to protect him and render aid.

"You're under arrest, Angus." Storm's voice was stern.

"Ain't happening, copper. You have nothing to charge me with." Angus's hand was hidden from Storm.

"That we do. Kidnapping, unlawful confinement, assault." Storm's eyes grew dark with his anger. How had Teagan survived, he wondered?

Shouts suddenly broke out as Angus raised a knife and plunged it into Storm's abdomen. Storm's forward movement stopped abruptly as shock and pain covered his face, a hand going to his abdomen. He pulled it back and stared at the blood on it, not hearing the yells for Angus to drop the knife. On his knees, barely able to stay upright, Storm felt himself fading from the scene, darkness blocking his vision. He didn't feel the knife as it once more plunged into his body, this time his back before he collapsed, his eyes closing as he lost consciousness. Storm didn't hear Angus taken to the floor and then handcuffed, hauled to his feet and then out of the door. He didn't hear the calls for paramedics, didn't feel the hands on his body as his fellow officers desperately tried to stem the flow of blood from the wounds. Storm just didn't hear, just didn't feel anything.

Rushed away to the Emergency Department, Storm's life hang in the balance as he was worked over in a desperate manner, each member of the healthcare team doing their utmost to save his life.

Will stood in the hallway, his eyes on Storm. He prayed for the younger officer, afraid for his life. He could hear the low voices and the comments. He knew the physicians who were being called in. Please, Lord, let him live. That's all I ask, is that he lives.

Turning away, his phone came out. He knew that he had to call Philip and Belle. This was a call that he always dreaded making, a call to a close relative. There had been many over the years. But some hurt worse than others. This was one of them.

"Will? You're calling?" Belle's voice held dread. "Storm?"

"I'm sorry, Belle. Storm was injured on duty this morning. He's here in our hospital. They're working on him. One of the physicians will be calling you. I just wanted to let you know that he's here."

"How bad?" Belle could hear Philip on his phone, could heard the distress and fear in his voice.

"It's bad, Belle. He was stabbed twice, trying to free Teagan."

"Teagan? Do you have her?"

"We do, Belle. What can I do for you, other than pray for you two right now?"

Belle shrank back against Philip as his arms came around her, sorrow in her whole being.

"I don't know, Will. We'll call the other kids and then head that way. Please? Keep us updated?"

"I will, Belle. I'm sorry." Will pocketed his phone, turning to find out where Teagan was. He needed to talk with her parents next.

Belle turned in Philip's arms as Storm's parents clung to one another. They had always feared something like this but prayed that it never happened. Philip stood back after a while, his hands out to lead Belle to a seat in the kitchen, her cup of tea in front of her.

"We'll need to head down there, Philip. But you have those meetings scheduled." Belle was worried.

"I know. I talked to George after I spoke with the surgeon. He's looking after that for me. He told us to go and not to worry about what's happening here, just to let us know what they can do for us."

"A surgeon?" Belle's hands covered her mouth as fresh tears started.

"A surgeon. He was knifed in the abdomen and the back. How much damage was done they can't tell until they get in there is how he worded it."

Chapter 24

His hand resting on the window, Davy stood in Teagan's hospital room. He studied the few clouds that were drifting across the night sky, momentarily blocking the moon and the stars. He sighed to himself, something that he thought he was doing a lot of lately. Teagan had roused briefly just a bit ago but had refused to say anything. In fact, she had refused to look at Davy, not even acknowledging that he was there.

Will hesitated as he approached her doorway, knowing that Davy was waiting for her to awaken. He had spoken with her parents earlier, just to see how they were. Her mother was a wreck, that he knew and fully understood. Her father and brother were angry and eager to talk with the one who had kidnapped her and held her hostage.

"Davy?" Will's voice was quiet as he walked towards Davy, his eyes on Teagan. "Has she been awake?"

Davy nodded, his eyes on Teagan and then on the doorway as he heard the hushed sounds of a late night hospital ward.

"She was, just briefly. She didn't say anything or even acknowledge the nurse speaking with her." Davy blinked hard for a moment, his tender heart getting the best of him. "Her mom helped her to clean up, the nurse said. That would help." Davy hesitated to ask.

"That's good. It will help. It will take time, Davy, for her to trust enough. This will have broken her to some extent."

"It will. Old Bill was around." Davy shook his head. "He was watching for her the whole time as were the other people on the streets. Storm has many friends out there."

"He does. Even though he's an officer, he made sure that his friends and people were taken care of. That's who he is." Will paused, knowing that he had to continue, but unsure how to.

"Storm? How is he, Will?" Davy looked at his chief, catching the sorrow briefly crossing his face.

"He's in the ICU right now. The surgeon was able to stop the bleeding but he lost a lot of blood, Davy. It's still touch and go. The abdominal wound nicked his bowel and hit the spleen. The back wound was more shallow, just into muscle. It will take time for him to heal."

"It will. The question then will be whether he comes back or not."

"That it will be. His parents are here. They're refusing to leave. And Peter and Paige have been in and out. Those three are close."

"They are, Will. That they are." Davy walked away, heading for the waiting room. He wouldn't be leaving there that night, not at all. Even though there was an officer standing at her doorway, he just felt danger approaching Teagan.

There had to be two parties involved, didn't there, Lord? How do we find out who is who? And somehow I think there's someone else. It just gets better and better, Davy thought sarcastically.

Will stood for a few moments, praying for both Teagan and Storm, his eyes on the young woman as she slept. Teagan had pulled the blankets up as tight around her neck as she could get and curled up in as small a ball as she could. He shook his head. His thoughts mimicked Davy's. Who all was involved and how they did find them before any more harm came to these two? And he would need to find somewhere that they could heal.

Will walked from Teagan's room, his steps slowing as he approached the two men waiting for him.

"Bruce? Barnabas? You're here?"

"We are, Will. Can we find somewhere to sit and have a coffee? I think the coffee shop is still open. We need to talk." Bruce pointed towards the elevator. "We need to discuss what we can do to help. Davy is a good friend to our people."

"He is. He worked his hardest on Dallas and Deri's adventure. And Storm certainly saved her."

His hands wrapped around his mug, Bruce Carey watched his friend. Will is disturbed and worried, I can tell. Lord, this is where You need to step in, isn't it? You will use the Barnabas Foundation once more.

"Will? I know you can't share specifics, but what can the Foundation do?" Bruce spoke at last, sharing a look with his son.

"Thanks, Bruce. I know they have been worried and trying to come up with something." Will sipped at his coffee, not really tasting it before he set his mug back on the table in a careful manner. He was thinking hard. "Storm's parents? If we could find someone to step in for his church? I spoke with their board chair. They can manage for this Sunday, he said, but they would need an interim even if just for a couple of weeks. He wanted Philip and Belle to be with Storm."

"That we can do. Buckley and Locklin have packed and headed that way with the Board's blessing. He volunteered as soon as he heard." Buckley had been the minister of their local church until he resigned to take on a new position with the Foundation. "Now, as to accommodations?"

"They're with Paige, Philip said. That will work, but we need to bring people alongside of them. This is where the Foundation steps in as always."

"We will. All of the men and ladies in the Building have come forward and volunteered to be here for them. So have their families of the ones who have them. Breck's parents and uncle and aunt are also on board with that. In fact, I think Beck and Bonnie were here with Philip and Belle."

"That's good. They know them well from years ago." Will was thinking past the present moment. "We'll need to see about Teagan's home."

"It's been taken care of, Will." Barnabas spoke up. "Our guys are looking after that. A house plan has already been drawn up and ready for Teagan to approve when she can."

———

Will nodded. "Your fellows are always ahead of us, aren't they?" He grinned briefly.

"They do that, Will. Teagan's folks?" Barnabas frowned for a moment, his eyes on the man standing in the doorway, seeming to search the cafe before he moved on.

"We're looking after them as well. Storm seems to have claimed Teagan, even if he hasn't acknowledged that as yet." Will shook his head at Barnabas.

"No, he hasn't, I don't think. He's been that worried about her, though. We've talked." Barnabas wouldn't divulge their conversations.

Chapter 25

Her senses letting her know that she was safe, Teagan roused, her eyes opening and then closing against the shafts of sunlight finding their way through the window. It was just as dawn was breaking. She listened but didn't hear the sounds of her captor coming for her, to yank her to her feet and drag her all over as he had been doing. Quiet footsteps stopped beside her and she jumped as she felt a hand on her wrist. The fingers were gentle which surprised her.

Her nurse had watched from nearby as Teagan had roused. Knowing what she had gone through had made Sue cautious as she approached Teagan, not wanting to scare her. She walked away, stopping just outside of the doorway to look back. Sue gave a sad smile. Teagan's eyes were open but she wasn't moving, almost as if she was too scared to do so.

"She's awake?" Ed, the officer on duty, spoke quietly.

"She is, Ed, but she doesn't want us to know that she is. It will take a lot for her to trust again." Sue blinked for a moment. "I've been friends with her for years. I just don't know how to reach her." She walked away to carry on with her duties, Ed nodding at her words.

Teagan roused even more, turning on the bed, staring around her. *This is weird, she thought. A hospital room?   How and when?   I don't remember coming here.   And that man would not have brought me.   He told me that.   He has to be here somewhere. He told me that I would never be free of him.   That it was Storm's fault.*   Teagan swiped at the tears on her face, worried about Storm.   She was trying hard to come back up from the darkness that she had been driven into.

Davy stood for a moment in the hallway before his feet carried him towards Teagan.   He frowned when she jumped as she heard his footsteps.

"Teagan?   It's Davy.   You're safe."   Davy's voice was low, but Teagan still heard him.   "You're safe.   We have you.   A guard is at your door.   The man is under arrest and won't be out soon."

Teagan barely looked up, unable to get beyond the fear of looking at the man.

"It's okay, Teagan.   We know that you're scared, beaten down, whatever emotion that you're dealing with.   I know someone who can speak with you."   Davy's hand rested on the sidebar of the bed. "We'll need to get your statement.   Can you tell me what happened?"   Davy waited, knowing that it would be difficult for Teagan to speak.

Teagan finally shook her head.   She couldn't.   If she did, then Storm would be hurt.   And that she couldn't allow.   Not at all.   He had worked his way into her heart.   Only she refused to believe that.

"Storm was hurt yesterday, Teagan, in getting you to safety.   We need to know what happened.   And we need to know now."   Davy was abrupt with her, not how he usually spoke.

Teagan's eyes flew to his, distress in hers.

"Storm? He's hurt?" Her voice was rough from disuse. She didn't think that she had spoken in the last ten days or so.

"He was. He's in ICU, Teagan. We need to know what the man wanted." Davy waited, almost impatiently. He could hear footsteps approaching and looked to see Old Bill standing there. He frowned at him.

"Teagan? You need to talk to Davy." Old Bill was almost in tears. "You need to tell him what happened. That man is a monster, as the kids say. You need to help keep him off the streets or he'll come after you and hurt you worse. We know that he beat you, that he broke you. Please, Teagan? Talk to Davy."

Teagan's eyes had remained on Davy as Old Bill spoke. She opened and closed her mouth several times, unable to find the words that she needed.

"He beat me, Davy. If I spoke, he slapped or hit me. He said Storm needed to pay. That I was Storm's woman and he wasn't going to let me go. That Storm would look for me and never find me. Then, he started making me walk around the streets with him. I don't know why." She blinked back tears. "Please? Is Storm okay?"

"No, he's not, Teagan. He was stabbed yesterday. He had to have surgery, life-saving surgery. Right now? He's in the ICU. The surgeon doesn't know if he'll make it or not." Davy watched with compassion as tears rolled down Teagan's face.

———

118

"Can I see him?" Teagan's voice was a mere whisper.

"Talk to me first, Teagan. Then we'll get you there." Davy's eyes held compassion even as he pulled out his lap top and portable printer. "Here. We'll set this up and you can talk." He watched as Old Bill walked away, a stoop to his shoulders that was not usually seen. Everyone's hurting with this one, Lord, aren't they? Davy's attention went back to Teagan.

Chapter 26

Packing his printer back into his case, Davy watched Teagan closely. Giving her statement had taken almost too much from her, he thought. Now what, Lord? She's asleep again. He turned, his briefcase and printer case in his hands and walked away. Teagan really had not been able to say much.

Davy was puzzled. Why Storm? And just what did this Angus want from him or Teagan? There had to be something there. He shook his head as the elevator door closed behind him, his eyes on the ceiling. What did Storm do or see that caused this? There has to be something.

Turning from the counter in the break room, Will opened his mouth to speak, then snapped it closed. Davy was there, reaching for his inevitable mug of coffee. A puzzled look was on his face.

"Did that Angus say anything that you know of, Will?"

Will had not been expecting that question but he knew that he should have.

"Not a word. He hasn't even asked for a lawyer.

"Then, why? Teagan wasn't much help. She really shut down after the first couple of days."

"She did?" Will frowned, his thoughts going to the resources available for her. "Who can we get her to talk to?"

"Burnie's Muir might be a good one. As to a professional, we'll need to find someone who can give us a report for the records." Davy was searching just who that would be.

"I know of a lady. She doesn't do it much any more but she has helped us in the past. Darcy Foster. I can call her but it will likely be better if you approach her. She's retired and has a craft shop now. Long story there for her. She knows what it's like to be on both sides."

Davy nodded, a long look shared between the two men.

"Thanks. I'll do that. Any word on Storm?"

Will shook his head.

"I spoke with his dad. He's still not rousing. Philip said that they have him on strong pain meds and are keeping him sedated for now. He's still intubated." Will prayed for his friend, petitioning for his return to health.

Davy paused, his own prayers rising.

"That sucks, you know, big time. And we have no idea why."

"And we have that other situation with Teagan. How's that coming/"

"It's not. I'm missing a single piece of information that would move it ahead. I've talked with Jace at Trackers. He's working on it, but they have a number of urgent investigations on the go. He suggested that I talk to an Evan and see if he can help. He works remotely for Emma."

"I would hold on to that for now. Dallas has been in touch. He's working it as he can and thought he might have a line on what was happening. He still has his own contacts in the area that he's reaching out to." Will walked away, his mug of coffee forgotten on the counter.

Davy sank into his desk chair. He was exhausted. The investigation with Teagan and Storm would need to be set aside, he knew, just because he didn't have that tidbit of information he needed. He stared at his open door before he reached for his phone, checking his voice mail and then diving into the workload on his desk. Davy looked up a few hours later, a frown on his face. A thought was niggling at the edge of his memory but he just couldn't draw it to the forefront. He sighed. He prayed once more for his friends and for their families, knowing that they needed that.

A few minutes later, Davy stared at his computer screen. He had been searching for any more information on Angus and what had appeared had shocked him. He was on his feet, looking for Will and not finding him. He paused in the hallway, a hand on his head before he searched the building for the officer who had brought in Angus, not finding him either.

This is strange, Davy thought. There has to be something here. He walked from the building, heading for a diner downtown that he liked to frequent. He often had notes and other information left for him with the wait staff. Hoping this was the case this time, Davy slipped into the booth that he favoured, nodding at the waitress as she poured his inevitable cup of coffee.

Davy watched the diners closely, seeing one man who was very interested in him. This is him, isn't it, Lord? How do we do this then? I need to bring him in. Only it doesn't work out too easy.

Walking away from the diner and then into an alleyway, Davy waited. He nodded his head, a grim smile on his face, as he heard footsteps following him. A hand on the man's arm had him handcuffed and being led to to a patrol vehicle. Davy watched closely before he headed away from there. He was confident that this man had answers. Only, how to get them from him was the question?

Chapter 27

Teagan tossed restlessly as she slept. Her dreams were haunted by the man who had kept her captive. She knew that he was in jail but it just didn't seem to matter. She awoke, her eyes searching the room before she breathed a sigh of relief. She was free and still in the hospital. Teagan sat up, not sure what had roused her.

Her mother watched her carefully before she walked towards her from the doorway. Amy hesitated as she did so, not sure how to approach her daughter any more. Davy had spoken at length with Tully and herself, shocking them with what Teagan had undergone.

Teagan stared in fear at the woman in front of her before she relaxed. Her mother was here and shouldn't be. She knew that Angus had threatened her family, her parents, her brother, and her sister. How he knew who they were was something that she just wasn't sure of.

"Teagan? How are you feeling today?"

Teagan simply shook her head. She had no idea how she was to be feeling. All she wanted was to be out of the hospital with Storm. Only that didn't seem to be happening.

"Storm? Have you heard how he is?" Teagan was desperate to hear news on him.

"I spoke with Belle. He's still in ICU, Teagan. She said they'd get you in today to see him." Amy reached to help her daughter sit up. "Here. Tara brought in some clothes for you. Belle said she'd come find us in about an hour."

Teagan moved to sit, her head swimming for a moment, before she was off the bed and grabbing the bag of clothes. She stared at herself in the bathroom mirror, hating the faint bruising that she could see.

Belle watched the younger woman walk towards her a while later, her heart praying for the younger woman. She didn't know where Storm and Teagan stood but she had watched her son, seeing the look in his eyes that said Teagan was special.

"Teagan? How are you, dear?" Belle simply swept Teagan into a hug.

"I have no idea. All I know is that I have brought danger to everyone."

"No, I don't think so. Storm was just doing what his job entailed that day and since then. Now, let's get you in to see him." Belle looked around, feeling watched. She frowned at the younger man who sat in the waiting room, trying hard not to watch them. *He's been there for so long, Belle thought. I haven't seen him going in to see anyone, now have I? Lord, we need Your protection. Guide us back to Your peace. Teagan needs it so much.*

Teagan stood, her hands gripping the bed rail, as her eyes sought the equipment around Storm. She paled as she realized that he was on a ventilator and a heart monitor as well. She didn't realize, she didn't think, that he had been hurt that bad.

"Belle?"

"Yes, dear? He's alive. This equipment? It's to aid in his healing. The surgeon is optimistic that he can be taken off the ventilator in a few days." Belle's arm was around the younger woman. "What were you told?"

"Not a lot." Teagan's brow furrowed as she tried to remember what Davy had said. "He was hurt when?"

"He made sure that you got away and then he was attacked. He was rushed here and had good care." Belle's emotions got the better of her for a moment. "Now, we have to leave, Teagan. We can only stay for a bit. But you can come back. We'll make sure of that."

Teagan nodded, her eyes on Storm, before her hand touched his cheek. She turned, almost running from the room, leaving Belle to follow.

Amy reached for her daughter, her eyes on Belle, who simply shook her head. What was going on with these two, neither mother knew. They weren't even sure if the two younger people knew themselves.

Teagan dropped to a seat in the waiting room, her strength spent for the moment. Her eyes found the young man watching her, a frown appearing on her face. She knew him, or at least she thought she did. But from where?

———

Chapter 28

The day that he was injured, Storm had made sure that Teagan was safe. He saw her rushed from the building by an officer and prayed that she would be safe. He needed to know that. Storm had partly turned from Angus to watch her leave, turning back in time to feel the knife sink into his abdomen. He had dropped to his knees, disbelief on his face, his hand first on his abdomen and then back into his line of sight, his face paling at the blood dripping from it. On his knees, his vision fading, he had barely felt the knife slicing into his back. He didn't hear the shouts from his fellow officers.

His fellow officers had rushed to his aid, a call going out for the paramedics. His suit jacket and shirt had been torn away as squares of gauze had been pushed hard against the wounds in an attempt to stem the flow of blood. The paramedics had moved in, working frantically on this as well as assessing him. They didn't like that his vital signs were fading.

Davy had stood and watched, praying hard for his friend and fellow officer. He saw the pasty colour of Storm's face, the whiteness of it, the blueness that was creeping into his lips and was afraid. Afraid that his friend wouldn't make it to the hospital or if he did, wouldn't survive even there.

The stretcher wheels squealing almost in protest at the speed it was being moved at, Storm was hurried into an examination room at the hospital. The trip in to there had taken hardly any time but the men and women were scared, to put it mildly. The physician and nursing staff had worked hard to stabilize him, to get him to imaging, and then to the operating room. Debris from their treatment littered the floor where he had been. They had all exchanged glances, not knowing if Storm would survive. It was the prayer of those who believed that he did and the hopes of those who didn't pray.

The surgeon had stood over him, assessing his injuries and then heading for the computer monitor where the imaging studies were on view. He shook his head. He really didn't think that Storm would make it. Not at all.

The surgeon and his team had fought for Storm's very life, at times almost losing him. The blood loss had been great, they realized. Dr. Watson felt other hands directing him as he worked. A believer himself, he knew that it was God who was doing that. That Storm's friends and family were united in prayer for him he also knew.

"Good work, team. I think that we've managed to stop the bleeding." He stood back, Dr. Watson did, his eyes on Storm. "Let's get him to recovery and then to the ICU. His family are here?"

"They are. They're in the waiting room. His parents were flown in from their home north of us." The head nurse helped to move Storm's stretcher to the recovery room.

Dr. Watson stayed with Storm for a good while, not quite sure if Storm would even make it. They still weren't sure if he would make it through the night. That was the prayer.

Walking away at last, Dr. Watson paused. Storm's surgery had taken a lot from him. Storm was part of the Bible study group that he belonged to. It hurt to see a young officer so gravely wounded. Storm wasn't the first one but it was different for him. Only Dr. Watson couldn't say why.

Philip looked up as he heard footsteps and rose, a hand out to shake Dr. Watson. Seth Watson was a friend of many years, and both Philip and Belle had been grateful that he had been the surgeon on call who had come in to operate.

"Philip? Can we get you and Belle anything?" Seth pointed back to the chairs.

"We're good, Seth. What can you tell us?" His arms were around Belle and Paige, a hand touching Peter's shoulders.

"You have been praying. I felt those prayers." Seth waited for a moment and then spoke. "He's in critical condition, as we talked about earlier. We have been able to stop the bleeding. The bowel has been repaired. Storm lost his spleen. The injury to the back was muscle. I would say that he was already collapsing when he was hit there."

"That's what they say. Now, can we see him?" Belle was adamant that she was not waiting any longer to see her oldest son.

"Shortly, Belle. I'll let you all go in for the first time. Then, you'll need to take turns. He's still in recovery and heading for a bed in the ICU soon."

"Thank you, Seth." Philip remained where he was, his thoughts on his son. Pictures of Storm through the years flooded his memory, from when he was first placed in Philip's arms as a newborn, through his curious toddler days to school days. He prayed for his son, looking up as he heard footsteps.

Will stood for a moment, assessing the four in front of him and then sitting. It had been a long day already and it was far from over, even though twilight had come.

"Philip? Belle? Do you have word?" Will's quiet voice barely broke through the stillness in the waiting room.

Philip nodded, his eyes closing for a moment.

"He's in recovery, Will. God kept him alive. Seth was just out." His eyes opened as he looked at his friend. "Any news on why?"

"That we're working on. We have his assailant in custody but he's not talking." Will gave a small grin as Peter snorted. "Peter?"

"That's what they always do, isn't it? Not talking? What can you tell us?" Peter was pushing and everyone with him knew that.

"Not a lot, Peter. I'm sorry. You know we can't. Any information has to come from Davy, not me." Will watched the younger man closely. "Don't go out there trying to find information, Peter. These people are brutal. Don't put your family through what they are now with Storm."

Peter nodded, knowing that Will had read him correctly. He would be out there searching, on his

own, and in danger. He felt his mother's hand on his
and nodded once more. He would stay back and safe,
at least for now.

Chapter 29

Two days later, Belle stood once more beside her son. The intubation tube had been pulled and he was breathing on his own. But he had still not awakened. That worried his mother. Belle was sure that Storm should have awakened. She turned as she heard soft footsteps approaching her, reaching out an arm to draw Teagan to her.

"Belle? Has he been awake?" Teagan's voice held her fear.

"No, he hasn't. Not yet. They expect it in a few days."

"I was praying that he had." Teagan reached out a tentative hand to touch Storm's face, finding him turning his head towards her hand. "Did he just do that?"

"He did, Teagan. He did." Belle looked at her son and then at the young lady standing beside her. "He's connected to you, even unconscious." Her arm tightened around Teagan. "Now, what can we do for you?"

"For me?" Teagan was surprised at the question. "I'm the one who's responsible for him being hurt. Both times. Why would you ask that?"

"Because Storm has been worried about you. He's talked to both his dad and I. And I think he's also talked to your family. We want to help keep you safe."

Teagan frowned for a moment.

"I'm not sure how you can even do that. I'm not even sure how to keep myself safe." Teagan was away from Belle, leaving the older lady to stare after her.

Pacing the waiting room, Teagan was disturbed, to put it mildly. How could she stay safe and keep Storm away from her? She just knew that once he was awake and on his feet, he would not stay away. Davy had been around, talking with her, going over what information that he had. And unfortunately, that was not a lot. Will had just sat with her, not saying a word, knowing that no words were necessary. Her family had been there on and off as had Storm's. She just didn't know what to say to anyone, not any more.

Teagan stared at the young man who sat, his eyes watchful. She frowned once more. He had been there on and off for a while. She rose, walked towards him and then sat beside him.

"Do I know you?"

He shook his head.

"No, you don't. But Storm does. My name is Brownie. I'm an officer from another town. I'm just here to watch out for you."

"I don't get that. Why?"

"Why? Because Storm is a friend of mine and others of my friends. We want to help you stay safe."

Teagan sighed, her head going back against the wall.

"But you work. You can't stay here forever."

Brownie laughed.

"No, I can't. I'm leaving tomorrow but others will be here. Evan, Tag, Shay, Dougal. All are or were officers and are friends. They will rotate in and out as they can. It's what we do, Teagan, if I may call you that. That's what we do for friends. It's how as Christians we are the hands and feet for God."

"That's an interesting way to put that." Teagan stared ahead of her, a thought crossing her mind. "Do you know what had happened to me?"

"I do. Storm had talked to me and the others. That's why we're watching for you. I have spoken with both Davy and Will. They are aware that we'll be here for you." Brownie nodded towards the door to the ICU units. "How is Storm?"

"Storm? He's off the ventilator but hasn't roused as yet. I'm scared, Brownie. What if he dies? It will be all my fault."

"No one thinks that, Teagan. He was doing what he was trained to do, trying to keep you safe. He wouldn't have done anything different." Brownie paused for a moment. "A mutual friend asked about him, just in passing. She has a business where she tracks people and finds information. She is working on that and sending anything that she finds on to Davy. She'll likely be around at some point to meet you and talk with you."

"Oh, she can't. It's too dangerous." She glared at him as he laughed. "What's so funny?"

"Her husband has a security team that trains other teams. He'll make sure that she stays safe. Emma and Abe do this for friends."

"But I can't afford to pay her. I just know that." Teagan showed her distress at that thought, knowing it would be very expensive.

"It's okay, Teagan. She doesn't charge friends. And she considers Storm and you friends." Brownie looked up as he heard footsteps and then was on his feet, a hand out to shake that of the man who walked towards him. "Micah? You're here?"

"I am." Micah, one of Abe's team members, grinned for a moment. "Emma sent me. Kat wanted to come but she had something on." He looked past Brownie. "And this is Teagan?"

"It is." Brownie turned, reaching to draw Teagan to her feet.

"Teagan, this is one of Abe's men, Micah. I would suspect that Emma has sent him on ahead with information."

Micah grinned again.

"That she has. Please, Teagan? Would you sit? This will take some time." Micah watched closely, seeing the stress that she was trying hard to hide. He prayed for her, that she would find peace, and that she would heal from this. He and his team members had been through what they termed as "adventures". Micah had almost lost the love of his life when Kataleen had been abducted and then left for dead.

Chapter 30

Teagan stared at Micah, not sure if she could trust him. She sighed to herself. *God, this is hard, do You know that? I don't trust as easily or as readily as I did. He broke me in that, dear Lord. He took away that aspect of my life that I valued. How do I get that back as well as the peace that disappeared?*

Micah watched Teagan, his eyes narrowed before he nodded. *She's struggling, Lord, isn't she?*

"Teagan? Emma sent me here with information for you. I will leave it with you to go over. She's put in her business card and asked that you call her when you have read it. Brownie can help." Micah stayed for a while longer before he apologized and had to leave.

Brownie watched Teagan closely, seeing just how near to breaking once more she was.

"Teagan? Let's look this over, okay? And then talk about it. If I know Emma, she has forwarded a copy to Davy as well."

"She has?" Teagan's eyes closed. Her emotions were just too high at the present time and that distressed her. "Brownie, do you know anything at all?"

Brownie shook his head, compassion on his face.

———

"They won't tell me, Teagan. I'm not involved in the investigations. And there is more than one investigation on the go."

"I know. I just want this over. Storm shouldn't have been hurt." Teagan blinked rapidly, not wanting Brownie to see that she was in tears.

Brownie smiled, a compassionate look once more on his face.

"It's what we do, Teagan. We put ourselves out there to protect our people. That's what he was doing with you. And going into that building as he did? That's what we do as well."

"I know." Teagan stared at the folder Micah had left with her. "Do I really want to see what's in this?"

"You need to, whether you want to or not. It will contain information that will help to keep you safe." Brownie sighed to himself, his eyes on the woman who had just stepped off the elevator. She doesn't belong here, he thought, his phone out to snap a picture of her and to forward it on to Davy.

"Brownie? What's this?" Teagan held up a sheet of paper. "What is she saying here?"

"What's that, Teagan?" Brownie reached for the paper, his eyes on Teagan first and then dropping to read what Emma had sent. "This? This is a summary of what Emma has found, combined with what Jace likely has found out as well. She's good that way, Teagan. She'll give a concise summary and then provide the proof that she has found. She states nothing unless and until it's proven."

"Okay. So, what does it all mean? I don't know those names." Teagan stared across the room, seeing her mother and Belle heading for her. "Here come the moms, Brownie. You take this." She tried to shove the folder at him, his hand up to stop her.

Brownie shook his head, refusing to take it from her.

"No, you keep it. Talk to Davy about it. And to Storm when he's able to."

"You really think that he will be able to?" Teagan's look held up even as she despaired of that ever happening.

"I am confident of that, Teagan. God isn't done with him yet." He watched as she swallowed hard, knowing that she was blinking back tears as well. "You care for him. That much I know. And I know that he cares deeply for you. It devastated him when you were missing and he couldn't find you. Talk to him, Teagan." Brownie had kept his voice low enough that Teagan was the only one who could hear him. "Belle? How is Storm? I'm Brownie, a friend of his."

"Brownie? Of course. I didn't expect to see you here. This is Teagan's mom, Amy. Now, what were you two up to?" Belle reached to hug Brownie, thinking that all of her son's friends were so tall.

"This." Teagan held up the folder. "Apparently, Storm has friends that I don't know about and she sent information for me." Teagan blinked rapidly before she frowned. "How did she know who to look for?" She glared at Brownie as he began to laugh. "It's not funny."

"No, it's not, but in a way it is. The look on your face is what we see when Emma becomes involved. She has a way of tracking and finding people that she can't explain. They're good at their work. I have a couple of friends who have gone to work for her on a remote basis. They both tell me that Emma is the best that they have seen at her investigations. And her husband's security team? The best that I am aware of, up there with a couple of other teams. And yes, if they are needed, they will be called in." Brownie simply shook his head at her. He tapped the folder. "How be we see what she says and then make plans? And here is Davy." He looked up with a grin on his face once more. "Emma's been busy."

"I see that." Davy's look said it all. "She's finding things and people once more that we didn't even know we needed to find."

Teagan's mouth dropped open at that, the two men laughing at the look on her face.

"If you don't know you need to find them, then why does she?"

"It's what she does, Teagan." Davy dropped into a seat near her. "It's how she does it. She can't even explain herself how she does it. She remembers people and events from years ago and then can tie them to an investigation."

Chapter 31

Rising at long last, Teagan walked away from the waiting room, heading for the stairs and then down them. She walked through the doors of the hospital to the outside, her face raised to feel the sun on it. Just where she was heading, she had no idea. The file that she had been given was clutched in her hands. Teagan stared at it for a moment and then searched the area surrounding her. For once, she didn't feel as if she was being watched but she was certain that she was. Only she had no idea who was after her now.

Tully watched Teagan for a moment, his heart breaking for his daughter. Just how he could help her, that he was not sure of. Not any more. All he could do was pray for her and trust God to keep her safe. Only he wanted to wrap her in cotton wool and stick her away somewhere safe, until this was all over. But Tully knew that would not happen. Teagan had changed, he knew, but he also knew that she would not rest until she had solved whatever it was that was happening.

"Teagan? Just where are you thinking of heading?" Tully stopped beside her, his eyes on the traffic on the nearby street.

"Dad? Where did you come from?" Teagan's startled eyes found her father's face. "And I have no

140

idea. I was handed this." She held up the file. "Someone named Micah gave it to me. And someone named Brownie has been watching out for us."

"They have been around." He reached for the folder and then with a hand on his daughter's arm, led her to his car, tucking her inside and then moving to position himself in the driver's seat. "What is this?"

Teagan shrugged. "I have no idea. Just information, I guess." She reached for it, fear in her heart at what she might find but determined to solve whatever it was that she had become involved in. "Dad? What are your thoughts?"

"My thoughts?" Tully rubbed at his face for a moment, trying to sort out those very thoughts. "Revenge? Did you see something that you shouldn't have? Heard something? Something in some documentation that shouldn't have been there?"

"My boss? Was he doing something illegal?"

Tully shook his head. "Not that we are aware of. I've known him for years. I haven't heard any rumours about him." Tully's words slowed. "Now, his brother? That man has skirted along the edge of legitimacy for years. He was always like that."

"Could he have done something? Something that was blamed on someone else?"

"It's possible." Tully reached to open the file. "Let's see what's in here, love, and then we'll go from there. Davy will need a copy of this."

"I think he already has it. Micah muttered something about that." Teagan sighed, her head going down to rest against the window. "Dad, I'm scared."

"We know you are, Teagan. You are bathed in prayer as is Storm." He paused. "Just what are your feelings for Storm?" He watched his daughter carefully, seeing the puzzled look on her face.

"Storm? My feelings for him?" Teagan stared at her father. "Gratitude. Fear. I'm scared that he won't make it, Dad, and that worries me. He was hurt because of me." She blinked rapidly to clear the tears that insisted on clouding her eyes. "What were you asking, Dad?"

"You are a beautiful, bright, intelligent, warm and loving young lady. Our prayer for you is that you find someone who sees that and loves you enough to to spend the rest of his life with you. Is it Storm? It might be. It might not be. All we ask is that you pray about this situation and your feelings for him. Your mother and I know you well enough to see that some are developing. If he is the one that God has planned for you, then we welcome him into our family. At present, however, we need to get through what you're facing. That's the difficulty, isn't it?" Tully paused to pray, knowing that he had to ask a hard question. "What are your feelings towards the situation that you're in?"

Teagan nodded, thinking through what had happened. Davy had asked her that as had Brownie. She had just stared at them, not willing or able to answer.

"About this? Guilt. Terror. Fear. Uncertainty. I feel as if God has walked away from me. But I know that He hasn't and won't. I'm afraid for Storm, that he won't recover." She stared into at the parked cars, not sure what her father was asking. "Personally?   I respect him, Dad.   He is compassionate, caring, aware of how I am feeling and tries to make me feel safe. Only, I wasn't. And I don't know what that man wanted." She blinked rapidly against the tears.

"It was revenge, plain and simple, love. He wanted to hurt Storm. He had seen you two together, thought that you were a couple, and it went from there. Davy's not saying why and that's only right, considering what the investigation is."

Teagan turned to stare at her father, seeing a look in his eyes that scared her.

"Don't do anything, Dad. I can't lose you."

"I won't, love, But let's take a look at what you have. Maybe these old eyes will see something that will help." He reached for the folder, his eyes on his daughter. "Never forget, Teagan. God is here. He surrounds you with His love and protection. It means that you have gone through things, will go through things, but He is there."

"I know that, Dad. It's just it's hard sometimes to remember that."

———

Chapter 32

Storm's eyelids flickered as he slowly roused, not sure where he was or why he felt so weak and in pain. He didn't remember what had happened. He groaned as a hand was raised to rub at his face, feeling the stubble that was on it. He frowned, thinking that was odd. Hadn't he just shaved?

His eyes moved as Storm took in the room he was in. Another groan came from him. The hospital, he thought. But what did I do? Storm tried to raise himself up but pain and weakness kept him from doing just that.

Storm slept, his body demanding that of him. Teagan watched for a moment before she reached to rest a hand on his cheek. Her thoughts were troubled. It had been a week since Storm had been hurt and he was only now awakening. She knew that he had been awake before, just not sure where he was. Her prayers were raised for her friend as she now thought of him. *Lord, please heal him? I don't know how I would take it if he didn't make it.*

Late that day, Storm's eyes opened and stayed open. He shifted on his bed, finding it hard to get comfortable. A hand found his abdomen and the bandages there. His head going back on the pillow, his eyes found the window as he watched the brilliant colours of the sunset fill the sky. Storm had spoken with the surgeon and knew just how close it had been for him. The surgeon had simply stated that Storm was a lucky man, staring at him as Storm shook his head.

"It was God, doctor. Plain and simple, it was God."

The surgeon covering for the original surgeon had shrugged and then walked away, to turn and stand in the hospital room doorway, a thoughtful look on his face. He didn't think that he had ever had a patient so severely injured who had healed so quickly. Storm would be going home in a couple of days, that much he knew.

Storm worried about Teagan. He needed to see her and had asked his father to find her for him. His heart hurt for his lady as he now began to think of her. When did that change, Lord? When did she become that important to him? His eyes slid closed as he prayed, not hearing the soft footsteps that approached. Storm jumped as he felt a hand touch his face and then he heard Teagan's prayer.

Teagan stood and watched Storm as she prayed for her friend. He had become important to her, important enough that she needed to be near him. She didn't want to acknowledge to herself that she was falling in love with her rescuer, certain that he would never return her feelings.

Watching her closely, Storm finally reached for her hand, startling her. His grip tightened as she tried to free hand.

"Teagan? You're okay?" Storm's worry was evident in his voice.

———

"I am. But you're not." Teagan chewed at her lip, a new habit that she had picked up. She had lost some of the confidence and feistiness that she was know for. That man, as she termed him, had done that to her. She was in constant fear that he would find her again. Teagan sought God in her prayers and her Bible, to find her way back to herself. Only, as Brownie had calmly stated to her, she would never be that person again.

"I'm okay, Teagan." Storm reached for the controls to raise the head of the bed, not releasing Teagan's hand. "You're struggling, Teagan."

"I am. I don't understand why he took me and then hurt you." Teagan stared at the window and the darkening sky, watching as the clouds scudded in front of the full moon.

"To get to me, I suspect." Storm's free hand raised as Teagan opened her mouth to protest. "I know who it was and what he is capable of. I had run-ins with him when I was on the street. He's been watching me over the last few months. When he saw us together, his mind warped. He thought that we were a couple and taking you could and would hurt me."

"He was? That's not good." Teagan pulled her hand free and wrapped her arms around herself as she began to pace. She spun to stare at Storm. "Where's God, Storm?"

"Right here. He has promised never to leave or forsake us. He didn't state that we would only have good times. God knows the path that we walk and what we face. He has already good ahead of us in this."

Teagan studied the man in front of her. She was beginning to know his character. Their lives had become entwined without either one of them knowing just how much that had happened. Teagan's sigh seemed to rise from her very toes. Storm's hand was reached out for her once more. She studied it and then sighed once more. *God? Where are You? Is this Your will for me? Is Storm the one?*

"What have you been told, Storm? About the situation from my work? I have spoken with Davy but he hasn't much more information on it." Her hand was clasped tight in Storm's by that point. Her eyes clouded with memory and pain.

Storm shook his head, his own eyes showing his concern and grief. Yes, he thought, grief. This beautiful lady has become involved in something and that something is still hidden.

"Davy hasn't said much but he's drowning in investigations. He's still working on ours. He said Emma from Trackers has been sending him information that he's working through."

"Micah from there brought information but I don't understand it." Teagan frowned, hearing a faint nose. "Storm? Who's in the room with us?" She spun, a small scream torn from her before her hand was torn from Storm's.

Teagan was pulled away from Storm, a hand wrapped around her mouth and an arm around her abdomen, holding her captive. She struggled but to no avail. She could not break free from the man holding her.

Storm shoved against the bed, reaching to throw back the covers, his motions stilling as a weapon was pointed at him. His eyes flickered to Teagan, fear coursing through him.

"You're coming with us." The man holding the weapon spoke in a coarse, rough voice.

"No, we're not." Storm focused on him, the periphery of his vision catching Teagan's struggles to escape.

"But you see, you are." A bag was tossed at him. "Get dressed. We're leaving in two minutes, whether you've dressed or not."

Storm's hands rested on the bag, his eyes not wavering from the man. The cocking of the revolver drew his fear to the surface and then his training kicked in. He reached for the curtain, drawing it around the bed. Storm struggled to dress, pain driving him to pause many times. The curtain was drawn back at last, and he searched for Teagan, not seeing her, only seeing the man holding the weapon on him.

"Where is she?" Storm's calm voice hid his fear and concern for his lady. "I said, where is she?"

"She's waiting for you. Now, let's move." The weapon pointed at the door and then back at Storm. "We're leaving here and now."

Storm's hesitation was brief before he gave an abrupt nod and walked slowly and cautiously to the door, opening it and then walking towards the elevator. His steps were hesitant and shaky as he tried to stay upright. He disappeared from view, not seeing his brother stepping from the other elevator.

Peter stared at his brother's bed, a frown in place, before he spun and almost ran for the nursing station.

"Where's Storm?" His frantic words caught the attention of the charge nurse who stared at him.

"In his room. He didn't have any scheduled tests today." She moved past Peter, to stand by Storm's forsaken bed, a hand reaching for the hospital gown. "He was here fifteen minutes ago. Teagan was with him." She spun and ran for the nursing station, calling for security.

A search by the security guards revealed nothing. Davy had appeared, concern for his friend and fellow officer bringing him there. A hand on the security guard's arm and a quick word had the two men rushing for the security office.

"There." Davy pointed to the video feed. "He's leaving the hospital. But who is he with? The man is hiding his face." Davy was frustrated. Storm and Teagan had disappeared once more but why? And who? That wasn't clear, not at all. His sigh shook him even as he took the package of still photos from the video feed that had asked for.

"Davy?" Will's voice held puzzlement even as he stared at the detective.

"They're gone, Will. Someone got to Storm and he and Teagan are gone. I have photos of them leaving the hospital but the abductors' faces are hidden."

———

Will slumped back in his chair, a hand drawn down his face. Fear and concern wafted through him and his thoughts went to the families. They didn't need this, he thought.

"Do what you need to there, Davy, and then head in here. I'll speak with the families once we've had more of a chance to talk."

"Peter's the one who discovered them gone. You can be sure that he's already contacted their families." Davy felt the frustration growing within him. He had headed for Storm that morning, a question that needed answering from another investigation uppermost in his mind.

Chapter 33

Teagan's heart pounded in her chest, fear threatening her very being. She struggled to escape the hard, tight grip on her arm and was just unable to. She twisted and turned, tugging at her arm, grimacing at the pain. Her fear was for Storm and no matter how she looked for him, she just didn't see him.

The youth, for that was what he was, roughly shoved Teagan into a car, sliding in beside her and slamming the door. His grip didn't loosen on her wrist. If anything, it tightened as she struggled to reach the other door and shove it open, desperate to escape.

The youth watched her, a smug look on his face. It had gone much better than they thought, catching Teagan and Storm on their own. Walking out with them had been a piece of cake, he thought. Not one person had questioned them. In fact, there hadn't been anyone around to watch. His gaze turned towards the front passenger door as it was yanked open and Storm was shoved roughly inside and down on the seat. Storm was unable to contain the groan as the pain hit him hard from the sudden landing on the seat and from walking out of the hospital under his own power.

Storm could hear Teagan's protests and cries to leave him alone as his vision darkened. He drew in deep breaths, his eyes sliding closed as he struggled

———

to stay alert and conscious. Storm felt Teagan's hand briefly touch his shoulder before the jostling of the car darkened his vision once more. Losing the battle to stay awake, his eyelids slid down and he slumped unconscious.

Teagan's scream filled the car until she was shoved to the floor, a foot resting on her back to hold her there. Terror overcame her as she vaguely heard the man and youth talking. A name that they mentioned tickled at her mind and memory before her thoughts changed to Storm. *Please, dear Lord, let him be alive. Don't let this set him back in his recovery. I don't understand why or who they are. But You do, don't You? You knew this would happen. I just wish that You had chosen another route for this.*

Teagan struggled to control her tears, unable to as they rolled down her face. She swiped at them angrily. *This was not her,* she thought. *I don't cry like this but it seems that's all I've been doing lately. Her eyes were on Storm, worried that he had been hurt even more. She tried to pray but her prayers seemed to go nowhere. Where is this peace that Storm talks about? I don't have it right now, Lord, and I need to.*

Fifteen minutes later, the car pulled into a garage of a house near the edge of town. Teagan frowned for a moment. No, she thought, they can't be involved. They're too prominent in town and in our church. She was yanked from the car, the grip on her wrist as tight as it had been. Teagan was forced through the door into the house and then down the hall to a room near the back. She was shoved forward abruptly, barely keeping her feet. She spun, her mouth open to protest, as she watched the man drop Storm's limp body to the floor and then stand watching her, a hard look in his eyes and on his face.

"You're here for now, little lady. The boss wants to talk with you. Your boyfriend may live if the boss likes what he hears."

Teagan stared at the door as it was slammed closed and the lock snapped shut. She was in shock, she thought, before she spun, dropping to her knees beside Storm. Tears once more clouded her eyes as her hands reached to roll him to his back. Her right hand touched his face, willing him to awake. But it was to no avail. He was unconscious, pain driving him down into that dark well.

Hours passed, with Teagan alternatively sitting close to Storm, his hand in hers, or with her pacing. She was terrified, she admitted to herself. She knew God was there but it was difficult to trust. Her head was having trouble with that.

Storm's head moved restlessly. His eyes flickered but he did not come up from that well of darkness. Teagan's voice broke as she begged him to.

Darkness was settling in as Teagan rose to her feet and felt for a light switch. The light was not real bright but bright enough that she could explore the room that they were held captive in. She opened doors, finding first a walk-in closet and then a small ensuite. Teagan stared at it and then back at Storm. She reached for a wash cloth and wrung it out in as warm as water as she could handle and slipped back to kneel beside him. She wiped at his face, her hand resting on his cheek, finding that he turned his face towards her hand. Teagan sighed, her eyes rising to the ceiling, prayers flooding from her.

Teagan rose and made her way to the bed, turning to stare back at Storm. She sighed to herself, not sure that she could raise him enough to get him on it. She stared at the bed, reaching suddenly to pull the pillows and then tugging at the mattress, pulling it to rest beside Storm. She dragged off the blankets and then dropped to her knees beside Storm.

A hand shook him, Storm rousing somewhat. He blinked and then looked around.

"Storm? Can you raise yourself up and onto the mattress?" Teagan reached to help him sit up and then raise himself to the mattress before he looked around.

Storm struggled to his feet, Teagan's hands reaching to steady him. He looked around once more and then headed for the ensuite. Teagan watched for a moment and then turned back to face the door as it opened. She frowned as she stared at the man, not knowing who he was. A tray was almost slammed down on a small wooden table, the force shaking the water bottles and sending them tumbling to the floor, where they rolled for a moment before stopping.

"The boss will be here tomorrow. Both of you will talk." The man glared at her, an evil presence being felt strongly as he backed away and slammed the door, the lock clicking solidly in place.

Storm stood for a moment in the doorway, hands gripping the door frame. He was on his feet but for how long, that he wasn't sure of. He watched

Teagan as she reached to pick up the water bottles, a sigh rising from within him. He knew the man who had abducted them, a contract killer. Fear rose within him. Storm knew that he was in no condition to protect Teagan or to defend himself. That was a given.

"Teagan?" Storm's voice was low and pain filled.

Teagan turned, concern on her face, a water bottle held in each hand. She tossed them to the table before she approached him, her hand out to touch his arm.

"Storm? What can I get for you?" She turned to search the room. "Not that I can get you much. They have left a bottle of pain killers."

"That works." His arm wrapped around his abdomen, he stumbled as he walked towards the mattress and then dropped down on it. "They left food?"

"They did." Teagan chewed at her bottom lip. "Sandwiches and water. I'm not sure that you can eat that or that you should."

"I can." He watched as she retrieved the tray of food and then reached for her hand, to pull her down beside him. Storm kept her hand in his as his head dropped. He drew in some deep breaths before he began to pray, seeking peace in the situation for both himself and Teagan.

Teagan paused as she unwrapped her sandwich, her eyes on her hands. She was conflicted, she knew, wanting to find that peace that Storm had prayed for but not sure that she could. Storm watched out of the corner of his eye, even as he twisted off the cap from a water bottle.

"Teagan? What's going on? What's happened since we got here?" Storm's head still hung down, his eyes on the floor, the sandwich held in a slack hand.

"Not a lot. The monster has been around. You know? The one who made you leave medical care?" She frowned as her head turned towards the door. She knew him, she thought, only she didn't know how. "He said that the boss wanted to speak with us. Only, who's his boss?" Teagan waited, not looking towards Storm.

Storm set his unwrapped sandwich down and instead loosened the cap on the water bottle. His thoughts were troubled. How did he do this? He was locked up and certainly in no condition to get away or even help Teagan get away. Recapping the bottle, he sat for a moment before his eyes closed. Storm slumped back to the mattress, a groan coming from him. *Lord, I can't do this,* he prayed. *I can't protect my lady no matter how much I want to. Please, dear Lord? Protect the lady that I love.*

Hearing a groan, Teagan spun, her mouth open to speak before she snapped it closed. Storm was gone again she thought, before she knelt and raised his feet to the mattress, reaching for the blanket to tuck around him once more. Teagan's hand rested on his cheek, feeling the stubble under it. She stared across the room, her thoughts troubled and tumbling over one another. Teagan knelt for the longest time before she began to pray. She was afraid, no, terrified, she thought, and needed help. Only the help that was available to her wasn't. Storm was sleeping or unconscious, which one that was, she wasn't even sure of any more.

Night darkened the sky and the stars and moon shone in all their glory. Teagan finally sought her own rest, her head on a pillow as she tried to get comfortable on the box spring before she stared at Storm. She had pulled a light blanket over herself. At long last, her vigil came to an end and she slept.

Neither occupant of the room heard the lock click as a key was turned in it and the door swung silently open. The boss stood in the doorway, his eyes intent on Storm and then Teagan. He gave a nod and then swung the door closed once more, the lock clicking into place. He had then, he gloated, and soon they would be put out of their misery, he thought. Storm had information that he needed as did Teagan. Threatening one would make the other talk, he decided, as he walked back down the steps and to the dining room. Sitting, he reached for his wine glass and then his fork and knife. Nothing like this interfered with his meals or his drinking.

Chapter 34

To say Davy was frustrated would have been an understatement. The photos that he had retrieved from the security video feeds were not of much help. The two men kept their heads down or with their ball caps pulled too far forward for any law enforcement officer to identify them. Davy had a sinking feeling that he knew them and that wasn't good. That meant they were involved in more crimes than just this abduction.

Will had been around as well, discussing the case in depth with Davy and anyone else who was involved in it. The level of frustration and fear for the couple was rising with each hour that they were missing.

Davy sat at his desk for the longest time the day after Teagan and Storm had disappeared. He was jotting down notes, his eyes rising every once in a while to stare at the wall in front of him. Hearing a tap at the door, he looked around.

"Dallas?" Davy rose to shake the hand of Dallas Chisholm, a recently retired detective. Davy was slightly older than Dallas, who had left the force to take up a new position with the Barnabas Foundation. "What brings you around?"

"Storm. I know you can't say much, but do you have any word?" Dallas sank into a chair, his eyes not leaving his friend and former partner.

———

Davy shook his head, frustration evident. He rubbed at his forehead with a thumb and finger, a headache beginning behind his eyes.

"Not a word. Not since they were marched out of the hospital in plain sight."

"That's worrying, isn't it?" Dallas paused, not quite sure how to proceed. "I had someone approach me last night when Deri and I were out for dinner. Someone Storm knows from the street." He held out the folder that he had held. "Here is the information that I was given as well as anything that I could find. They are truly in danger, Davy, if the man who I think has them really does."

Davy shot him a glance as he took the folder. Dallas would not be here if he didn't have information that he had confirmed. He opened the folder and read through the material, before he flipped back to the beginning, his pen out to mark and comment on the pages. Davy sat back, a frown on his face for a moment as he thought through the material. His eyes raised to find Dallas studying him thoughtfully.

"This man?" At Dallas' nod, Davy slumped back into his chair for a moment before he was pulling his computer keyboard towards him. Working through passwords he pulled up a program, entering the name. His heart dropped for a moment as he read the man's rap sheet. "He's brutal, Dallas. We need to find him."

"I know, Davy. I just don't know how we do." Dallas' finger tapped at the arm of the chair. "The building guys are working it as they can. Storm has become a friend to them and they want to help. The ladies are working it as they can." He paused, a thought crossing his mind. "I wonder if Fynn can help." Fynn, wife of his friend, Brady, was a forensics entomologist and thought differently from others, just given her work and her experience.

Davy looked at his computer as it chimed for a new email. He grinned suddenly.

"Fynn is at work. She's sent information that she has been able to find. She has also called in Emma and Abe."

"Now, things will go ahead. I know Emma had been working on it. She had sent Micah with information for Teagan. Did she share that with you?"

"Teagan didn't, but Micah was around. It is an interesting read." Davy leaned forward. "I worked those streets, Dallas. I have no idea where they would be kept."

"In town, likely where we would least expect to find them. A well-to-do area, I suspect. If the man that I think it is has become involved, he is not cheap to hire." Dallas uttered a name of who he suspected of hiring the abductors, raising Davy's eyes to him. He nodded. "Him. I had a run-in with him when I first started on patrol. He is an evil man, to say the least." He rose, pausing for a moment, his eyes on the fingers that he was rubbing together. "We need to find them, Davy. Only I don't know how we can. The building fellows are looking and word is out on the street that the Foundation wants them found."

"That will help." Davy rose as well, walking to the front doors with Dallas, stepping through to walk down to the sidewalk. He squinted against the bright noonday sun. "How's Deri?"

"She's good. Worried about Storm. After all, he did save her life and she feels that she owes him." Dallas bit at his lip, not sure how to continue. "She's making a list, she said, of those she suspects. I think she may be on to something."

"She knows her town. Going through what you two did, she'll likely figure it out. And I suspect that her father and brother will become involved." Davy shook a finger as Dallas grinned. "They already are, aren't they?"

"They are, as much as they can. She's talking with the building ladies and thought she would have a list in the next day or so." He pulled out his phone as it dinged and then grinned at the text message. "She's sending you a list, Davy. She's named someone." Dallas tilted his phone for Davy to read the name.

"Him? Oh, man! We'll have difficulty providing that." Davy frowned at Dallas as he grinned once more. "What are you thinking?"

"I'm thinking that Emma is already aware of this man and is deep into research on it. Or else Evan is." He mentioned a friend of Storm's, who had retired as an officer and gone to work for Emma on a remote basis. "They'll find the information that we need."

"I know. She'll send me more than I need." Davy was grumbling and they both knew it, but they both knew that Emma was thorough in her investigations and could find information and people that others could not. Emma could not explain how she did it, only that it was how her brain worked. They were in awe of her memory and how she could pull people and details and facts from the deepest recesses of her mind.

Davy watched as Dallas walked away before he turned to head back into the department building, pausing as a thought came to him. Instead, he turned and walked towards the downtown area. He was dressed casually that day in jeans, sneakers and a sweatshirt and would not stand out in the area that he headed for. A quick purchase at a diner and he headed for a favourite bench, sitting and then sipping at his coffee. He knew that he had been seen and that someone would approach him shortly, if it was safe. That was a given. Davy had reacted the very same when he worked the streets. He knew his people there. Even though he was not undercover at present, they still contacted him with information and names. That, Davy prayed, would be the case today. He felt time was running out for his friend and his lady.

Chapter 35

Davy had finished his coffee, the cup tossed into a trash can beside him, but he stayed where he was. He had spied the youth watching him from across the street and nodded. He had been seen and someone would be along soon.

A few moments later, a seemingly homeless man slid down on the bench, his clothes, although clean, worn and torn in some places. He didn't look directly at Davy, keeping his head and eyes down. Davy shoved the second cup of coffee towards him as well as the bag containing the sandwich that he had chosen. The man wolfed down the sandwich and then gulped at his coffee.

"What do you have, Sam?" Davy's voice was barely audible, his gaze on the movement of the pedestrians and the traffic on the street.

"He's got them, Davy." Sam was an undercover officer, well known to Davy. The two had worked together before. "His home on the other side of town. He's brought in hired muscle. Word is that one of them is a contract killer. That can't happen to Storm."

"No, it can't. But we can't go in without evidence that they are there." Davy puzzled over what he knew and what he could actually do. "Keep me informed, Sam. You know where to leave word for me." Davy was on his feet, moving away, his thoughts troubled as he determined to find the information that they needed to free Storm and Teagan and obtain the search warrants that would do just that.

Sam watched as Davy walked away, knowing that Davy could not act, but the street people could. He rose, a determination in him to save his fellow officer and his lady. There was no doubt in anyone's mind that Teagan was that, no matter how she and Storm had connected. Sam had watched them from afar, had watched Teagan when she was held captive, and then watched as the investigators and officers searched for Storm.

Standing near the building where he knew Storm was held captive, Sam studied the area and then the building itself. He knew that very few men were there. He had seen the man known as The Boss as well as his underling and the youth. There didn't seem to be more people than that, he thought. Sam would keep watch, waiting for an opportunity to enter the house and free his fellow officer. That much he knew.

Days passed, one after the other, until it was day six. Sam watched as the businessman left, his henchman serving as his driver. He saw the luggage that was placed in the trunk and then turned his eyes towards the house. This may be his opportunity to get in and out. Only, it would not be exactly legal, he knew, if he went in. A voice spoke from beside him.

"We'll go in, Sammy. You stay out." Leo, a friend from the streets, a former drug addict who had turned his life around and now worked with the local mission to help those who lived the life that he had been drawn away from.

"I can't let you do that, Leo." Sam was torn, knowing that he had to try to free Storm and Teagan but knowing that he would not be on the right side of the law if he trespassed to go in. He didn't have solid proof that they were even there.

Late that night, Leo moved towards the house, his eyes watchful as his head twisted to spy out the area. He had friends with him, ones who walked the legal line but who knew Storm and wanted to help him just as he had them. They didn't tell what he had done, but each one knew that they had a debt to pay to him and this was their chance.

The younger of the men with Leo reached for the door, turning the knob, surprised to find it turning under his hand. The door opened slowly and silently. The boss would not tolerate any squeaking or creaking, that was a known fact with his employees. They crept in, separating to search each of the rooms on the main floor and then Leo and the youth headed for the basement, finding it unfinished, a surprise in the fact. They crept back up the stairs and headed for the second floor. One of the older man returned from the garage. They searched the second floor thoroughly before they crept back down and out of the house.

Leo turned to stare back at the house. Storm and Teagan were not there. They had found the room where they had been held captive but no sign of them. The mattress was back on the bed and the bed made correctly.

"What happened, Leo?" The youth spoke for the group of men and youths. "Where are they? They were there, we know. I didn't see them taken out of there." Surprise and shock coloured his voice and his face.

"I have no idea." Leo stared at the house once more. "I know. He has another house close to here. Let's go there." He was away, almost on a run, the men with him on his heels.

Leo slid to a halt, a hand up to stop the rest of the men. His head turned as he searched. There were low lights on in the house.

"We need to plan." Leo crept forward, the group following him. "If they are there, we need to find that out before we go in."

"We do." The first youth, Eddy by name, volunteered to go to the door. "Let me see what I can find out." He was away before anyone could say anything.

Eddy knocked at the door, shifting from foot to foot as he waited.

The woman who answered the door kept it halfway closed, a hand on the knob to close it quickly if she needed to.

"Can I help you?" She frowned in distaste as she studied Eddy.

"I need to find work. I am young and ready to do anything. Do you have some that you could hire me for?" His grin lit up his face but not his eyes. Those were narrowed as he studied her and then what he could of the hallway. He frowned for a moment as he saw multiple pairs of shoes cluttering the mat near a closet. They were the wrong size for her, he thought, and not what someone who lived there would even wear. Men's shoes and ladies' shoes? They might just be here.

The woman frowned, closing the door for a moment. Eddy could hear voices from behind the door before it was pulled open and the woman reappeared.

"Be here at 8 a.m. tomorrow. You can work in the yard." The door slammed in his face as he stared at her. This had gone much better than he had even hoped.

Eddy's eyes sought the sky as a thoughtful look crossed his face. He turned to walk slowly back toward Leo, puzzled that he had been hired.

Leo stared at Eddy as he told him that he had been hired to do yard work in the morning. He then stared at the house. *Was this God? Had He done that?*

"What was that, Eddy?" Leo's attention turned back to the youth.

"There are a lot of pairs of shoes in the hallway. Shoes that don't suit the house." Eddy turned back to the house. "I think that they're there somewhere. But how do we prove it?"

"That we will work on. I need to find Davy and talk to him. Only he said he would be in court the next few days." Leo was torn, knowing that he needed to do that and not willing to go near the police department.

———

A voice spoke from beside him and he jumped in surprise.

"I'll find him, Leo. Are they here?" Sam had approached them, the darkness of the area covering his coming.

"We think so, but we can't prove it." Leo was deeply worried about Storm and his lady. He felt it was only a matter of time until their bodies were found and that was not what they all wanted.

Sam nodded. "We'll work it through. Eddy, I'll be around here while you're working. Not in sight, but I will be watching you carefully. We don't need you to disappear as well."

Chapter 36

His hand on the diner door in the downtown area, one that he frequented regularly, Davy paused for a moment. His thoughts were on Storm and Teagan. Were they in that house? His team and fellow officers were frantically searching for enough information so that they could obtain the warrants that they needed and move in. He shook his head, watching as Sam approached and slunk by him to head for a booth at the back. Davy smiled. Sam had word for him or else he would not be here.

Davy's hand was raised to the diner owner as he followed in Sam's footsteps, sliding into the booth on the opposite side of the table. A quiet thank you came from him as filled coffee mugs were placed before him ad the waitress took their orders.

Sam maintained his demeanour of a down and outer, someone who society shunned. Davy waited, knowing that Sam would speak when he was ready. He would not be rushed. His thought turned to the number of cases that were waiting for him and sighed to himself. There was just too much work, too many cases, too many people hurting. Will was aware of that as was Davy's supervisor and were working to try and help alleviate some of the burden. Only, the solutions would take too long, Davy was privately convinced.

Sam looked up from under his brows, the intelligent look in his eyes belying his demeanour.

"They're not there, Davy."

Davy didn't let his surprise show.

"They're not? Just how do you know that?"

"Friends went looking." Sam refused to name them and Davy didn't push. "The house is empty. He and his man are away."

"So, we're starting over." Davy was down-hearted, having convinced himself that they would be found that day.

"No, not really. We tracked down another house. Someone is going to work for the woman who lives there. He said there were a number of pairs of shoes in the hallway that didn't fit the home."

Davy nodded even as he raised his coffee mug. He wouldn't pry, he decided. Sam would tell him who it was if he felt he needed to. Davy's trust was there with the people on the street. Most were good folks, just down on their luck, or running, or whatever reason it was that they were there. Some on the other hand were deep into crime. Those concerned him.

"You'll keep up apprised of anything. He'll be working outside but we'll have someone watching out for him and for Storm. We need to find him."

Davy agreed, his thoughts troubled.

"We do, Sam. Here, let me pay for our meal. Will wants to speak with you." Davy didn't look directly at him.

"He does? Tell him to meet me here at supper."
Sam was on his feet, shuffling away, the very picture
of a vagrant but his bright alert eyes were watchful.
He frowned for a moment as he spotted a man waiting
outside and then nodded to himself. He turned to
watch the man, quickly scribbling off a note to Davy
that he slipped into his pocket as that man passed
closely by him.

Davy noted the man as well and recognized him
as an accomplice of the man they were seeking. Why
he was down there and watching him? Davy gave a
grim smile. He was fishing, Davy decided, trying to
see who Davy was speaking with in an attempt to find
out what Davy was doing or more importantly who he
was after.

Eddy watched carefully that day as the woman
came and went. He was puzzled. She had hired him
to work outside but gave no orders. He had found
Leo earlier that day and questioned him. Leo had
pondered his question and then shrugged, stating that
he had no idea what she was up to, but Eddy needed
to be very careful.

Eddy returned for the next three days before he
came to work one day and found the woman gone and
the house doors wide open. That puzzled him even as
he entered and searched for his employer. He stood
in the rooms on the second floor and stared at the
debris. It confirmed that Storm and Teagan had been
there but no longer were. Eddy turned and ran,
heading for Leo, who called Sam.

Sam in turn reached out to Davy, who sped to
the scene with patrol officers. Something had
happened and it was directly related to his case.

———

Davy paused at the doorway of one of the rooms, watching as the crime scene techs worked. He turned as Will approached.

"Davy? Talk to me. What do we have?" Will studied his detective, trying to read his face and not quite succeeding.

"They were here, Will. I don't know when they were moved but it looks as if it was overnight. Now we need to find them once more." Davy was frustrated to say the least. "Sam knew who was working here and they got word to him. The woman was found in the garage. She's dead."

"Dead? Killed to keep her quiet?" Not much surprised Will much any more, not after all this time.

"That's what the evidence is saying. She was strangled." Davy shook his head, despair rising for a moment.

Will grimaced and then stared around.

"What evidence have they found so far?"

"Not a lot. There's garbage in the rooms that it looks as Teagan and Storm were kept in. I can't tell what condition they're in at this point." Davy turned away, frustrated and walked back down the stairs to the office. "The techs have gathered everything that they can and are working through it. Everyone is working overtime on this, Will, desperate to find Storm. He's been so instrumental in a number of our cases over the years in bringing the culprits to justice."

"That they are. And I have told them all to stop after a certain number of hours. I won't have any other cases or workloads disrupted, as much as we want to find Storm." Will walked away, his phone out as it chimed. He spun to search for Davy, heading his way again, a hand out to draw him from the house.

"Will?" Davy was puzzled. He was the lead investigator on the scene and needed to stay.

"Andy's taking over here for now. I want you with me." Will strode towards his car rapidly, Davy almost running to keep up with him.

"Will?" Davy almost didn't get his seatbelt fastened before Will had accelerated away from the area.

"I have word where they are. Sam came through." Will searched for the building that he was looking for.

"What?" Davy stared at Will and then at the surrounding area. "How?"

"I don't know all of the details yet. He's meeting us there." Will pulled to the side of the road and stepped out of the vehicle. Davy stopped at Sam's side, a puzzled look on his face. "Sam, talk to me. Are they here?"

"They are. They were moved here last night. Friends watched it happen and got word to me." Sam didn't let on that it was Leo and Eddy, who had been searching diligently for the pair.

"Anyone inside with them?" Will stared at the rundown building. "Or were they just dumped here?"

"No one is here." Sam shot a look at Davy and then Will. "We need to get to them. The owner of the building has arranged for it to be burnt down tonight."

Will paled. "Tonight? Let's go."

The men ran for the doorway, shoving open the door and rushing inside. They searched, not finding the pair.

Sam was puzzled. "This is where they were to be. Are there any secret rooms?"

"No. This is bizarre. Sam, what do your sources say?" Davy stared at him, watching as he thought it through.

Sam spun, eyeing the crowd. "I have no idea. Let me see." He slunk away, keeping his status a secret. He wasn't sure if he had even done that.

Will watched the scene, a frown in place. Where were Storm and Teagan? He was deeply worried and his prayers became more desperate. His gut feeling was that there was only a short time to find them and find them alive. And Will's gut feelings were usually correct.

Chapter 37

Storm twisted his wrists, trying to free them from the ropes that bound him to a column in the living room of the house that they had been brought to. He was worried about Teagan, watching her as best as he could. She had been quiet and withdrawn the last few days. In part, he thought it was because they had been separated in the last few days, unable to spend time with one another. He had begun to heal, but was still not back to his full strength. The deprivation that they had been privy to the last week or so (he had forgotten just how long) had not helped to heal or strengthen him.

Unable to free himself, Storm's head went back against the column and his eyes closed. He began to pray, knowing that he was unable to save himself or Teagan. Only God could do that, and right now, his trust factor was low. He prayed for peace in the situation and slowly felt it seeping into his heart and soul. He continued to wait, not sure why or what he was to wait for, but God impressed deeply on him that was his duty now.

Storm's head came back up and he searched the room. It was not an affluent house, somewhat run down. He was puzzled why they were there. It was the third place that they had been held in. The first place had been opulent and Teagan had been allowed to remain with him to take care of him. The second place had seen them separated, even as Teagan protested. He had heard her cries and sobs and tried his best to get free to her. That had not been possible.

This was different. Here they were tied up in the same room, albeit across the room from one another. Teagan's head was down, resting on her upraised knees. He didn't know how to reach her or how to comfort her. Storm had not recognized the men who had moved them, handling them in a rough manner. He had protested that for Teagan, but a blow to his face had stopped his words. Storm moved his jaw, finding it painful.

Teagan tried to stifle her tears. She was so afraid, more afraid than she had been yet. She had tried to stand up for herself, stand up for Storm, but had been handled roughly. The blows and strikes that she had taken had beaten her down, almost to where she had been when that monster had had control of her. She tugged at her bonds, not able to dislodge them. Her hands were tied behind her back, her wrists drawn through the back of an antique wood chair.

Darkness was settling in when Storm spoke. They had been brought there early in the day and just left there. He suspected that no one would be returning and he had little hope that his friends on the streets would find them. His head dropped back again and his eyes closed. As much as he wanted to stay awake and on guard, his body said otherwise. He slept, not hearing the soft, cautious footsteps that approached.

Teagan gave a squeak of fear when the men appeared, fear that they would be killed uppermost in her mind. A finger to the one man's lips stilled her words as she opened her mouth to speak. She felt her bonds loosened as the rope was cut.

"Don't make a sound, Teagan." It was Leo who spoke. He had tracked them down and was now working to free them. "We're friends of Storm's. We'll get you out of here." He rose to his feet once more, scooping her into his arms.

Teagan's arms went around Leo's neck almost without her thinking. She twisted to look over his shoulder, seeing that Storm was free and with arms over the shoulders of two men, was following her from the house.

Leo hurried them away, his head twisting as he watched closely for anyone who was coming. There was no one. That confirmed his suspicions, that Storm and Teagan had been left there, left to die. Their bodies would have been moved and buried somewhere no one would have ever found them.

Leo gently set Teagan on her feet and kept an arm around her to help her balance on her feet. Teagan's eyes closed and tears trickled down her face.

"Teagan? You're safe. We'll get you to somewhere safer soon." Leo looked around at Storm, finding the men helping him to lower himself to the ground. "Storm?"

Storm squinted through the fog of pain and discomfort.

"Leo? You're here?"

"I am, Storm. We've made sure that you and Teagan are safe." Leo crouched down beside him, a hand resting on his shoulder. "I'll get word to Sam and he'll get word to Davy."

Storm shook his head.

"That won't work. I heard them talking about Davy. They know he's looking for us. If he continues, they'll kill him." Storm's head went back as he stared up at the night sky. "Where can we go? They seem to have eyes everywhere."

"They do, Storm." Sam was there, how he knew no one ever figured it out. Sam simply said God had told him. "I'll get word to Davy. For now, we'll find somewhere to take you."

"Take me home, Storm. No more running. It doesn't seem to matter if we run and hide, they still find us." Teagan had slipped to a sitting position beside Storm.

Storm's arm gathered her close, his eyes on her face before he nodded.

"Leo, we'll go to my place. Sam, I'll need your help in the morning. I have a plan."

The men helped them to their feet and walked away with them. The youth who had been working at the home was sent to find Davy.

Davy stared at the youth before his hand was out and he drew the young man into his house. He stared at him, before he spun and paced the kitchen.

"They're safe?"

"They are. Sam asked me to find you. He said that they were taking them to Storm's house." Eddy watched Davy. "What can I do?"

"For starters, we need to make some plans." Storm's phone was out and he was calling Will. "Will? I have news."

"News? Storm and Teagan?" Will sat upright in his easy chair. He had been almost asleep, his wife having already retired. Will had felt something would happen that night. "They're okay?"

"Relatively speaking, they are. Eddy is here. Sam sent him."

"Eddy?" Will frowned for a moment. "Sam's involved?"

"He is. I don't know all the details. Eddy says that Storm asked to go home." Davy handed Eddy a bottle of water and pointed to the table, waiting as Eddy sat. "I'm not sure of that but Storm usually is right on with his instincts."

"He is. We can't head there tonight. And I don't want either of their families heading that way." Will was pacing, running scenarios through his mind, trying to make a decision that would keep them safe and solve the mystery that surrounded the couple and seemed to be growing.

"No, we can't. I'll track Sam down in the morning." He pocketed his phone, his eyes on Eddy. "Not a word about what you heard, Eddy. It could mean Sam's life."

Eddy, his eyes round with worry and surprise, nodded.

"I already figured out that he was a cop. Things would happen when he was around." Eddy gave a soft thank you for the sandwich that Davy handed him. "How can I help?"

"For tonight, you stay here. I'm going to need your help. You'll be the go-between for me. I can't go to Sam or those on the street. Not when Storm is safe." Davy paced, his mind working overtime.

"I get that, sir. But I do want to help. Storm's been good to me over the years. He's made sure I was safe, had somewhere to stay, encouraged me to finish school." Eddy drew himself up with pride. "I'm to enter police college in a month or so."

"You are? Congratulations. We can use good men like you." Davy gave a grin as Eddy drew himself up even straighter, a look of pride on his face.

Chapter 38

Storm paced his house, not willing to sleep. He reached for a mug of coffee, not sure at that point what number it was. He knew that Teagan was asleep. He had checked on her, standing beside her bed, a hand resting on her cheek. He felt the stickiness of her tears and his heart broke for the lady who he know acknowledged he loved deeply. A plan was forming in his mind and he turned to the computer, pulling up the information that he needed and printing off what was required. Storm wanted to wake Teagan up and talk to her but didn't. She needed to sleep and so did he. He sank into a chair in the living room and slept, not knowing that his friends from the streets were outside, keeping vigil and watching for those who meant Storm and his lady love harm.

Teagan sat upright abruptly, fear on her face, a small scream coming from her. Where was she? She scrambled from under the covers and ran for the door, hunting for the men who had kept them captive. A scream was torn from her as she felt hands on her arms. She struggled desperately, her hands hitting at the man, until she recognized the voice. Teagan threw herself at Storm, her arms tight around his neck as she sobbed in relief. She felt safe for the first time in days.

Storm held her, his arms tight around her. How did he keep her safe? He didn't know if she would go for his plan, but they had to do something. He finally scooped her into his arms, stifling a groan as he did so, and headed back to his chair in the living room. Storm settled himself, Teagan's head resting on his shoulder. He had heard from Sam, who would be there in about an hour or so. He squinted at the clock. It was only 5 a.m. but it felt much later. They would need to speak with their families, but he wanted to speak with Davy and Will first. Sam has said that those two men were aware that Storm and Teagan were free.

Speaking quietly, Teagan voiced her concerns.

"Where do we go, Storm, so that they can't find us? I don't know where we can."

Storm moistened his lips before he spoke. He had prayed and prayed about what he was about to suggest. He had not sensed God saying no and if he had had that, he would have set aside his own plans.

"We'll make plans, Teagan. But first, I need to talk. Just hear me out, please? This is something that I have prayed about over the last few days, particularly in the last few hours." He watched her face. "Will you marry me, Teagan? I love you and want to keep you safe. My prayer is that we spend the rest of our lives together."

Teagan had stilled her movements as he spoke and her head raised, her eyes on him. He turned to study her, finding her watching him.

"Storm? Are you serious? At a time like this?" She shoved at him, finding his arms tightening around her. "We can't! And I love you too."

"We can. I have had friends do this, marry quickly to keep one another safe. I can call them and you can talk to the ladies." Storm was serious.

"Okay. But when? I want my Mom and Dad there." She blinked rapidly to clear her vision.

"We can do that. I think we should do this soon, even today. I don't want to rush you, but I don't want to lose you." Storm was torn.

"Okay. Can we call Mom?" Teagan's hand rested on his, stilling his motions. "No, it's too early."

"No, I don't think so. I know my parents wouldn't be sleeping much. I doubt yours would be any different." He reached for his phone before he paused and reached instead to kiss her. "I have a ring that I hope you will like. It's a family heirloom. If it's not what you want, we can find another."

"No, it's okay, Storm. It's just so sudden. And we're still not safe." Teagan's face crumpled for a moment as she looked up, searching for answers that just didn't seem to be coming.

"We don't have to, Teagan." He groaned as he heard a knock at the door. "Here. You take my chair and here's my phone. Call your mom." He reached to kiss her again, reluctant to leave her but knowing he had to answer the door.

Davy stepped inside, his eyes finding Teagan as she huddled forward in the chair, her voice tear-laced and low. He then turned his attention to Storm. His eyes narrowed as he watched him watching Teagan. *They have made a decision of some kind,* Davy surmised. *Will they share it with us or not?*

"Storm?"   Davy's voice caught Storm's attention.

"Davy? Let's head for the kitchen. I haven't made coffee yet and need it." Storm paused, his eyes drawn once more to Teagan, finding her watching him before she glanced towards the window.

Davy slid back a chair at the kitchen table and dropped his files to the tabletop. He reached for food, stuffing bread into the four-slice toaster and then for eggs. This was something the two men had done before, prepared and shared a meal. Only this time? There was a lady involved, one who had Storm's heart and one who Davy was worried about.

Storm turned once more to face the kitchen door, not hearing Teagan's voice. He was deeply worried. He knew who was involved now and that man was a powerful force in the town but also in the deep underworld of crime. No one had ever been able to prove it. Storm sighed to himself as he reached to pour coffee for the three of them. It seemed that it was up to him to prove it, but how did he do just that and keep the love of his life safe? He would need to talk to his friends and see what they would suggest, the four friends who had been through danger with their now wives.

Davy nodded as he watched Teagan approach. She was wearing out and wearing down. This last abduction and confinement had done that to her. Teagan walked into Storm's hug, feeling that she had come home. She turned to study Davy, finding him watching her.

Chapter 39

Teagan kept shooting glances at Davy and then sharing looks with Storm. She was torn. How did they go ahead with their plans, given what they were going through? Her mother had not been surprised at what Storm has asked. She was just concerned at how quickly. Amy had promised to talk with Tully and then Thurlow and Tara. Amy knew what the reaction would be. They would support her, she was sure, but her father would have many questions for Storm.

Davy ducked his head to hide his grin. He knew Teagan wanted him to tell them it was all over. He kept their conversation light and shared a look with Storm. Storm just shook his head.

"Davy? Where do we stand in the investigation?" Storm finally asked.

Davy stared at him for a moment and then at Teagan. His hand reached for his mug, tipped it and then he rose to refill it. He stared out of the kitchen window for a moment, gathering his thoughts. He finally turned and stared across the room. Davy sat at long last, his hand resting on the top of the folders. He wasn't quite sure how to proceed.

"Davy?" Storm spoke, his hand reaching for Teagan's. "Before you start, we know who it is." He stated a name, bringing Davy's head around to watch him.

———

"Him?" Davy sorted through the paperwork in the files. "We didn't have that name. How did you connect them?"

Teagan shook her head.

"He is. I heard his voice and saw him. I am terrified of him, Davy. How do we stop this? And who else has he done this to?"

Davy nodded. That had been his own thought, that Storm and Teagan were not the only ones this had happened to. Sam had been muttering something along that line but he had no idea of names that they could investigate.

"Davy? Can we pray?" Teagan's voice held hope, despair, and fear, if that combination were at all possible.

"We can do that, Teagan. In fact, we need to. You need to find the peace that only God can give right now. We're coming up to where authors would say we're at the climax or the crisis or whatever word you would wish to use."

An hour later, Davy reached for the top folder, pausing for a moment. No, he thought, he was missing something and he didn't know exactly what it was. There was a crucial piece of information missing.

"Okay, before we start with this, you two, talk to me. Tell me exactly what happened and as much as you can remember. I know that you have given your statements." Davy's gaze flickered between the couple, who had turned to stare at one another.

"We can do that, Davy." Storm responded, a frown on his face as he stared at Teagan. She was getting angry, he could tell, and that worried him. Sure, he was angry himself but he knew that he needed to set it aside and talk with Davy.

Teagan blinked rapidly, her eyes on Davy. He was right, she thought. Anger was rising inside her and she refused to tamp it down this time. Forgive me, Lord. I just can't not be angry. This has disrupted my life and wreaked havoc in so many. Storm has been hurt because of me and had to go on the run. How do we solve this?

Teagan turned to Storm, finding him watching her. He nodded and reached for her hands once more. His thumbs rubbed along the back of them, Teagan watching him in turn.

"Davy? Who found us?" Storm was uncertain as to who it had been,

"Sam, but he didn't go in. Leo. Eddy was watching as well. I am not sure who all was there." Davy looked down for a moment. He knew who all had been there but he wasn't ready to share that information.

"Davy? This is what happened from my point of view." Teagan drew a deep breath. She was not ready to speak, not yet. There were many things, thoughts, happenings that puzzled her and that she needed to process. "Okay, so we were taken from the hospital room. I don't know how Storm managed. One man, no, a male in his late teens, took me out first and stuffed me into a car. I tried to get away but he overpowered me. He didn't let go of my wrist.

Storm came out and was shoved into the frost seat. I don't know how he managed to stay upright to get out there."

Teagan's thoughts drifted back to that day. What a horrible day, she thought. She and Storm had been talking quietly, not about much, when the men had appeared. She had been dragged out of the hospital to the car, struggling to escape. Storm had appeared, slumping down into the front seat and then seemingly to fade away from the scene. She was terrified, afraid that Storm would die.

They had been kept in the first house for two or three days. The man had appeared two times a day, bringing food and water. He had just stood and stared at Teagan, even as she begged for supplies and painkillers for Storm.

Storm had roused somewhat by the third day. But by that time, they had been moved, sent to another house. This time, the man had watched them more closely, aware that Storm was waking up. He had begun to make demands, only Teagan didn't understand what they were.

Chapter 40

Teagan had stared at the man, a frown in place. She knew him. He had been seen around town for the last year or so. Teagan wasn't sure what he actually did for a living but she was not getting a good feeling from him. Evil seemed to surround him. She looked past him to see the younger man standing in the hallway, eyes on Storm, a weapon in his hand down by his side. She grew even more afraid.

"What do you want?" Teagan's voice was fear-filled. She felt Storm's arm around her shoulders and leaned back on him.

Storm was not steady on his feet, the only thing holding him upright his arm around Teagan. He frowned as he too studied the man and then froze. He knew who he was. Storm was suddenly very afraid for Teagan. This man was muscle for hire and also was known to be an assassin. If he was here, then one or both of them would not be walking away.

The man stared at them and then down at his fingertips. He was puzzled by them. They were not what he had expected. Teagan had stood up to him on many occasions. That was not what women did when he confronted her. Storm? He was a different story. Assaulting an officer he knew would bring him to justice and that he wanted to avoid.

"You have information that we need. From your transcription work." His face hardened. It didn't matter to him that a woman was involved. He had killed women before and that would happen again. He had no remorse about that at all. It was just work for him.

"I don't know what you mean. I have no information."

"But you see, you do." The man walked away and then came back to stand inches in front of her, his hand reaching to grip her wrist in a hard manner. He refused to release it as she twisted and turned. His grip just tightened.

"I don't have anything you would want. Nothing! Why would anyone think that?"

Storm spoke, his eyes on the man.

"She's telling the truth. She knows nothing." His arm tightened around Teagan.

A hand was raised, and the man shoved Storm backwards. Storm lost his balance and fell heavily, landing on the side where he had had surgery. He didn't move for a moment, the pain and shock wafting through him and darkening his vision. He faintly heard Teagan's voice raised in anger.

At last, the man walked away, anger on his face, the door slammed and locked behind him. Teagan stared at it and then was across the room, on her knees, her hand reaching to help Storm sit up.

Storm's arm wrapped around his abdomen as he willed the pain to recede. He felt Teagan hugging him and reached to wrap an arm around her.

"It's okay, sweetheart. It's okay. I'm fine." Storm blinked rapidly and swayed for a moment before he stiffened his knees. "We'll get away. God is here, sweetheart, and will protect us."

"I know that, Storm. I just wish we weren't." Teagan walked away, searching for a way out of the room. "Why?"

"Do you know what he meant?" Storm stared at the floor for a moment, lost in thought, before he looked up and then walked over to stare out of the window.

"I have no idea. Nothing that I transcribed was suspicious. Just letters and some reports." Teagan paced, her hands gripping the hair at the sides of her head and pulling at it. "Nothing. I don't get it. Was I working for a criminal?"

"No, you weren't. I don't know why they think there is something there." Storm chewed at his lip for a moment before he spun, a finger pointing at Teagan. He had had a thought but needed out of that room to follow it up. He could only pray that one of his friends on the streets had seen them. He had no way of knowing that they had and were tracking them.

"Was my boss a criminal?" Teagan's brow wrinkled as she puzzled it out.

"No, he wasn't. I know that for a fact. There have been rumours about someone with the same name who is a criminal. He's not from this town though. I don't know how this connects to you. Davy may know, but we need to get away and talk with him."

A few days passed and then the man appeared once more, grasping Teagan by her hair and dragging her roughly from the room. She cried out in pain and struggled to escape. Storm was prevented from reaching her, an arm twisted behind him as he too was forced from the room. Shoved into a vehicle, they were bound and blindfolded. A short car drive later saw them pulled from the car and shoved forward, a hand to each one's back directing their steps.

Pushed to the floor, Storm felt the column behind his back even as he felt his hands bound behind him. He could hear a scuffling sound and Teagan's voice telling the men to leave her alone and to leave Storm alone and that she had no idea what they wanted. She never did.

Silence grew in the room. Storm struggled to release himself and was unable to. His head went back against the column and waited, for just what he didn't know. Teagan struggled to get out of the chair that she was bound to and just couldn't.

Time passed. There were finally soft footsteps approaching. Soft words were said, almost inaudible between the men and youths that had approached. Knives were produced and the bonds slashed.

Teagan was gathered into arms and rushed from the room. Storm was drawn to his feet and over a man's shoulders and he too was rushed out.

Teagan looked up at last to find Davy watching her and then watching Storm, his notebook on his knee, a pen in his hand. There was more than what they had said, he knew from experience.

"You described the men in your statements. Any further details?"

Teagan frowned for a moment.

"The younger one? I think he was still a teenager. But he was vicious. The threats that he gave? No one should ever have to heard what he threatened." Teagan shuddered at her memories. "I can't even put into words what he said."

Davy nodded, knowing what she was likely hiding. The youth had been found and arrested. The arresting officers had been threatened with violence and death.

"What else?"

Storm took up the tale, not sure that he could add anything.

"I know the voice of the man, Davy. He's a contract killer. He's been around town for the last few months. Leo has heard rumours that he has been behind some of the deaths we've had in the downtown area and in the outlying areas."

"That's the word we've been getting. We just don't have the information that we need to prove it."

"We need to find that." Storm's head dropped as he gave in to the fatigue and pain for a moment. "This needs to end, Davy, and now. Teagan may not survive if we don't."

"Davy? You've investigated my boss, didn't you?" Teagan was puzzled.

"We did, Teagan. He was in the clear, as we say. Nothing hidden about him or his children. The same for the others in the office." Davy was puzzled too. There just seemed to be something that they were missing, a link to something.

———

Chapter 41

Teagan thought back through the clients that she had seen coming through the office. A sudden thought had her drawing in her breath in a sharp manner, even as she gave a sharp cry and turned her face into Storm's shoulder.

"Teagan? What did you remember?" Davy leaned forward, eyes intent on her.

"I did. About six months ago, I heard raised voices in the office next to me. It wasn't my boss but his brother and someone else. I don't know why his brother, Ted, was there. He didn't work there. In fact, my boss didn't want him in the office. He just never explained. Could he be behind all this?"

"His brother?" Davy sat back, his eyes on Storm. "I'm not sure that we ever looked at him and we should have." His phone out, Davy was on his feet, moving away from them. He returned to sit back down in a few moments, frustration evident. "I'm sorry, Teagan, Storm. He was only looked at in a cursorily manner. I have asked him to be brought in and questioned."

"Are we safe?" Teagan was hoping against hope that they were.

"Not quite yet. We have to interrogate him, continue our investigation and go on from there." Davy was deeply concerned.

Storm nodded, knowing the process.

"We'll try and stay as safe as we can, Davy, but we are going to go on with our lives. We're not hiding." Storm kept his eyes on Davy, his arm tight around Teagan.

"We get that, Storm. We know that you just can't stop living."

Davy finally rose and left, Storm walking outside with him. Storm stood, searching the area. He could feel the eyes on him but just couldn't see them. Teagan stood in the doorway, watching him and then too searching the area, before she moved towards him and into his arms.

"Storm? Who's out there?"

"Someone is." He dropped a kiss on her forehead. "You talked with your mom?"

"I did. She said they'd be here this afternoon and were we sure." Teagan bit at her lip. She knew that she loved Storm deeply and that God seemed to be moving them together. "What about your people?"

"I talked to Dad earlier this morning. He said they'd come this afternoon as well. And he welcomed you to the family."

"He did? He was that sure?" Teagan was surprised.

"He did. He said that your feistiness was just what I needed, to keep me in line." He ducked the elbow that she shot at him. "I'm sure, Teagan. God is leading in this. He's here, right around us. He allows things to happen, things that we may wish never had, but we are never alone. He will give us His peace in all this.”

“That’s what I really don’t get.” Teagan leaned against Storm, feeling his strength of character in how he held her.

“Think of it this way. Remember how the disciples were so afraid in the storm until Jesus calmed it? He brought peace to the midst of the storm. That what God does for us. In the midst of our storms, He brings us His peace. We don’t have to like what we’re going through, but Jesus promised never to leave us or forsake us. That’s a promise that He will never break.”

Teagan shuddered in fear for a moment and then replied again.

“I have trouble with that right now.”

“He understands that as well. Just tell Him how you feel, just like you would your earthly father. He already knows that but He wants us to talk to Him and tell Him. That’s how He is our Father.”

Teagan turned her face up to watch Storm.

“Thank you, Storm. Now what?”

“Now what? We need to see about a license. You need to find a dress. We need to find a minister.”

“Do you know of someone other than our minister?”

“I do. There’s a little mission that I go to down town. The minister there is a good friend.”

"A mission? Oh, I've heard about that one and wanted to go but I didn't know how safe I would be."

"With me, you'll be safe. My friends will watch out for you."

Late that evening, Storm turned as he felt a hand on his back. Teagan had approached him as he stood on the back patio, watching the stars and moon.

"You okay?" Storm's voice was soft. He was still in awe that this beautiful lady had agreed to be his bride.

"I think so. You?"

"I am, sweetheart. You were so beautiful in your Mom's dress."

"She had saved it all these years. She was sad that we didn't have a longer courtship and that we married in a hurry, but she understood. She and Dad didn't have a long engagement either so they can't really say anything. Dad just asked if I was sure and that we learned to trust and love each other quickly because of what we had gone through."

"That's so true. Dad mentioned that as well." Storm just held her as she wept for a moment. "We'll get through this. Davy sent off a text just a bit ago. He wants to meet again in a couple of days. He has some information for us and asked that we just stay safe."

Chapter 42

Storm turned from the window a week later. He was healing but still not allowed to work. He was frustrated. He needed to be doing something and just wasn't able to. Teagan was standing in the doorway and held out her hand.

"Come on, Storm. Let's go exploring."

"Eploring?" One eyebrow was raised even as he reached for her hand.

"Yes, exploring. Let's go find some of your street friends and see what they are saying. If it won't put them at risk."

"It might but if I can track down Sam or Leo, that would work." Storm reached to lock the door and then taking Teagan's hand headed for his vehicle. "We'll search for him. Thank you, Teagan."

"Thank me? For what?" Teagan was puzzled.

"For being who you are. For not being afraid to face life and the danger that we're in. For wanting to find out who is responsible. For not being afraid to meet my street friends."

Teagan stared at him before she blinked and then gave a huge smile.

"You're right. That's who I am. I had forgotten. That man did that to me, driving who I am deep inside."

"He did and he is facing justice on that." Storm sighed as his phone chimed. He pulled it out and tossed it to Teagan.

"It's a text from Davy. Sam, is it?" At Storm's nod, she continued to read the text. "He wants to meet with you. How did he do that?"

"Do what?" Storm grinned at her.

"Know that you were looking for him."

"That's Sam. He's good." Storm bit at his lip, not wanting to let on to Teagan that Sam was in fact a police officer.

"He must be a cop." Teagan didn't look up so she missed the look of surprise and then understanding that flitted across Storm's face. "Davy said to find him in a diner."

"I know the one. Sam was responsible for finding you that time and then finding us."

"He was? I need to thank him in some way."

Storm shook his head as he searched for a parking spot, pulling into one just a block from the diner. He reached to open Teagan's door and then for her hand. He froze as he felt the eyes on him, bringing a puzzled look to her face.

"Storm?" Her quiet voice broke into his concentration.

"He's here, Teagan. We need to be very careful how we proceed." His phone was out and a text sent off to Davy. "He'll have someone come around and search. This man will be found and found shortly."

"Did Davy ever say anything about Ted?"

"Not yet, but he won't. We're the victims, Teagan, even though I am an officer." He held the door for her and then reached for her hand once more, leading her to a booth at the very back of the diner. He waited for her to sit and then slid in beside her, his eyes on Sam who has already arrived. "Sam."

"Davy! It's good to see you on your feet. And Teagan? How are you?" Sam's smile lit up his face.

"I'm not sure how to feel." Teagan frowned as he laughed softly.

"About how you should feel at this stage of the game." He looked up with a word of thanks as mugs of coffee were set in front of them.

Orders placed, conversation was light and general. Teagan kept looking between the two men, not sure what to expect or why they were talking as they were.

"It's okay, sweetheart. We'll talk more but for now, just bear with us." Storm kissed her cheek, causing her to blush. Sam just grinned at her. "It's how we do this."

"Okay. It just seems strange, that's all." Teagan bit into her hamburger and her eyes closed. "This is so good. I think it's the best I have ever tasted."

"They make their own meat patties. A family recipe that they keep handing down." Sam bit into his sandwich. "They're good to the people on the street. They feed them if they have no money or let them pay as they can. Not many do that. They're connected with the mission that Storm wants to take you to."

"He's right, sweetheart."   Storm pushed his empty plate aside and folded his arms on the table. "Okay, let's talk, Sam. What's up?"

Sam nodded, his eyes on Storm.

"He's outside now, Storm. Just waiting to take you out. You two escaped from him, and that has never happened to him. He's angry and wants revenge. He'll spare nothing to kill you two."

Storm nodded even as his hand tightened on Teagan's.

"We've talked about that, Sam, and know that is exactly what he will do. Davy was sending in officers to try and find him. I doubt that they will."

"No, I doubt they will. But I do know that he has no friends on the streets and no one is helping him. You are too well thought of, Storm, for that to happen. And that feeling transfers to the lady who you love."

Storm nodded, knowing that Sam spoke the truth. But where did they go from there? Davy had said that they were working through what they needed to and that arrests were imminent. But they had to finalize the investigation and then procure search and arrest warrants. They just weren't quite there yet.

Sam rose at last and shuffled from the diner, keeping to his street persona. He stood across the street, not watching the diner but watching those around. His eyes narrowed and then he reached for the cell phone he had secreted on his body. The assassin was standing in plain sight.

<hr>

"Davy? I have him in my sights. Outside of the Box Diner." Sam moved closer to the man. "Storm and Teagan are still inside there."

"Okay." Davy was on his feet, running for his vehicle, beckoning for Will to come with him.

"Davy?" Will fastened his seat belt at Davy pulled away from the curb outside of the detachment, lights on but not the sirens.

"Sam found the assassin. He's watching Storm right now."

"Where?" Will's phone was out, his fingers dialling Storm's number.

"The Box Diner. They need to stay inside or head out of the back door."

Will spoke rapidly to Storm, whose shocked voice echoed through the phone.

"He'll stay put, he says." Will pocketed his phone, reaching for the door handle as Davy slid to a stop. "Okay, where is he?"

"Sam said near the outreach centre. Just to the left of it." Davy walked quickly that way, Will at his side. "And there is he. Good. We have officers approaching him."

Davy walked up to the man, a hand reaching out to touch his shoulder. The man jumped and spun, his face hardening as he saw the officers surrounding him.

"You are under arrest, Jay Western. And wanted in multiple municipalities." Davy took great pleasure in slapping on the handcuffs and then handing him over to a patrol officer. "Take him in. We'll sort out everything soon."

Will looked around, finding Sam watching from a distance. Sam touched his forehead in a salute and then melted away in the gathering crowd. Will turned towards the diner as did Davy.

"Who gets to tell them?" Davy grinned as Will simply shook his head and walked that way.

Teagan watched closely as Will and Davy slid into the booth across the table from them and accepted with thanks the mugs of coffee placed in front of them. She shared a look with Storm, who simply shrugged.

"Davy?" Teagan could finally not control her curiosity. "What happened? Will calls Storm and tells us to stay put but not why."

"The assassin? He was outside waiting for you two to come out. You would have disappeared and we not likely would have ever found you two, at least no alive."

Teagan paled as Storm wrapped his arms around her.

"He was outside?"

"He was. Sam found him as he left." Will held up a hand. "That goes no further. You understand that?"

Teagan nodded and then sighed.

"Is it over yet?"

"Not yet. We still need to find out who was behind it. That we are working on." Will sipped at his coffee.

"And he won't talk. That much I know." Storm pulled out his phone as it vibrated and kept vibrating. He peered at the text message. "That's Emma. She sending you information, Davy, that leads to the one responsible. She hasn't said who but asked that you call her." Storm didn't mention that she was sending him the exact same information.

Once more at home, Teagan rose at last and walked away, to do what, she wasn't sure. Storm watched and then moved to his computer, drawing up his secure programs and searching. His face grew stern and then whitened as he read of the man who they suspected. He was in town and that was not what he wanted to hear.

Chapter 43

Two weeks later, Teagan paced the house. She was at a loss, wanting to work but not sure what she wanted to do. Storm had watched her earlier that morning, simply reaching to hug her and tell her that it would soon be over. Davy had promised that, and Davy was never wrong.

The doorbell rang and Teagan spun, a frown on her face. They were not expecting anyone, not that she was aware of. She paced quietly to the door and stared through the window, careful to keep to the side. Barnabas Carey? Why was he there?

"Barnabas?" Teagan gave a half smile.

"Teagan? I'm glad you two are home." He stepped inside, reached to hug her and then shake Storm's hand. "I've been meaning to stop by but Aubrey and I have been away."

"Come on through to the office, Barnabas. I have coffee just brewed." Storm pointed the way, watching as Teagan led the way.

Barnabas rubbed his hands together at long last.

"I felt burdened to come and speak with you two today. Buckley wanted to come but had to head in another direction. He still feels as if he's the minister of our church." Barnabas reached for the folder that he had dropped to the table beside him. "This is a proposal from the board. Teagan, we know that you are looking for work. Storm, you are heading back to the force? But not yet. This is a proposal for a new ministry that the board would like to set up, directed to the street people and those who are looking for full time work and aid. We have spoken with the mission Cadee's folks are involved in and with the church down there. They are thrilled to hear that this is a possibility. Teagan, we would set you up in an office down there. Storm, we would set you up as the liaison between them and whoever it is that they need to reach out to. It is not full time work for you, not yet. We would have others who would work under you. All we ask is that you pray about it, talk it over, and then let us know your decision. You both do not need to be involved or neither one of you need to be. Whatever you decide is okay with us." Barnabas spent some time in prayer with them and walked away.

Teagan stared after him and then at Storm, who simply wrapped her into a hug.

"What do we do, Storm?" To say Teagan was shocked would be an understatement.

"We pray about it. We covet prayers from our families simply asking for prayer about an offer of employment. We don't need to give any details." Storm was content just to sit and hold his bride.

Teagan relaxed against him. They spent time in prayer and then just talked quietly, getting to know one another. They had not had time to do that. Teagan finally walked away, leaving Storm to study his computer screen, trying to make sense of what they were going through.

A sudden sound had him reaching to close his programs and then jump to his feet. He stopped moving forward abruptly as his brother and Teagan's brother were shoved roughly into the room. Peter hit his knees, his hands out to brace himself from falling face down on the hardwood floor. Thurlow barely kept his feet, his hands raised in the air.

Storm stared past them, keeping his face closed and expressionless. *This was it,* he thought. *Lord, only You can get us out of this. I can't. Protect Peter and Thurlow. And my Teagan, my beloved, my soulmate. Wherever she is, protect her. If someone has to die, let it be me.*

"Where is she?" Ted Turney strutted into the room, his heavy form showing his lifestyle. "Where is that witch?"

"Witch? Who would that be? I am not aware that I am familiar with anyone that I would describe that way." Storm held his hands in the air as well, praying that Teagan had managed to escape in some way.

"Your wife. Teagan. Who calls anyone such a stupid name, anyway? Find her and bring her here." A weapon dug into Storm's side as one of the henchmen stepped to his side.

"I have no idea. The last I knew was that she was going to be in the kitchen." Storm was shoved forward, to search the house and then the outdoors. There was no sign of Teagan. He could barely keep on his feet with the violence he was subjected to. "She's not here."

Ted Turney shook with rage. He had been told by the man who he had watching the house that Teagan and Storm were both there. This was the day that it would end. That the other two men had shown up? Collateral damage was how he referred to it. He really didn't care if they lived or died.

Teagan had been walking the yard earlier when a neighbour had approached her, introducing herself and then asking her over for a tea or coffee. Teagan had stared at her and then smiling, had agreed, walking around the fence and to the back patio. A friend, she wondered? Carola and she had found that they had many things in common, reading a passion they both shared. A heated discussion on their favourite books had followed.

"How be you and Storm come for supper tonight?" Carola had greeted her husband, Tony, as he had arrived home. "It's no problem. We were planning on grilling."

"Oh, that sounds wonderful." Teagan had risen, then frowned as she stared at what she could see of the road. "I don't recognize that vehicle."

Tony had stood beside her, studying the vehicle. He was a prosecuting attorney and knew who the police were looking for.

"That's who they're looking for, Teagan. You can't go home. Carola, into the house and lock the doors." Tony waited until the two women had disappeared before his phone was out and he was called for help. He watched as the marked and unmarked patrol vehicles pulled up and officers moved towards the house. His prayer was that Storm was still alive and well.

Davy moved in with the officers, reaching for the front door and turning the knob. He knew that officers had moved to the back of the house and would be entering it from there.

Raised voices came from the office and Davy pointed that way. The officers moved forward, standing just outside the door as they listened to Storm and Ted speaking. Ted's voice was raised and angry. He really wasn't caring what he said. These three men wouldn't be alive by night, that he was certain of.

Storm caught a hint of movement in the hallway and a frown fluttered across his face. He nodded to himself. Teagan called it in after seeing something.

Davy moved forward on almost silent feet. His weapon pressed into Ted's back as his other hand grasped his arm and pulled him to a stop.

"You're under arrest, Turney. This time? You're not getting away." Davy waited until the man was handcuffed as were the others.

The officers hustled the men out even as others took the men's statement. Davy paced the house, moving to the backyard and then to the fence.

"Tony? We have them. Thanks for calling it in."

"It was Teagan. She just stated that she didn't recognize the vehicle. I knew that I had not seen it before on the street." Tony stared back at his house.

"Teagan and Carola were on the back patio, just talking. That saved her, didn't it?"

"It did. She would have died today as would Storm, his brother, and her brother."

Tony paled at the words.

"Their brothers? God was good, wasn't He?"

"He was. He protected them in a way that only He can." Davy looked towards Tony's house. "I'll need to speak with Teagan." Teagan was there as he finished his words.

"Davy? Storm?"

"He's okay, Teagan. So are your brothers."

"I knew that they were coming over. I just didn't expect this to happen. Is it over?" Teagan was desperate to hear that it was.

"It is, Teagan, except for the final interviews and to finish up our investigation." He looked around as he heard movement and saw Teagan launching herself at Storm.

Storm looked up and nodded, tears on his face. They were finally safe, he thought. God had brought them through the storm and gave them peace. Teagan moved from Storm to hug Thurlow and then Peter before moving to hug Davy.

Davy simply shook his head.

"We'll be back in a couple of days, you two, just to finish up what we can. Stay out of trouble, okay?" He laughed and waved at Teagan's cry that they did, it was everyone else that didn't.

Chapter 44

Teagan picked up the tray containing the desserts that she had prepared, knowing that their families had gathered to meet with Davy and Will. This was it, she thought. *This is when we find out why and what it was all about.* Storm reached to take it from her as she reached the living room doorway, handed it off to his father, and then pulled his bride into his arms. They stood for a moment before Storm dropped a kiss on her head and turned her to face the room. Standing there watching their families talk and laugh together, they could hear and feel the relief in the room.

"Did Davy give any hint at all of what he had found?" Teagan's voice was quiet. She was still in shock, she thought, that it was all over with.

"Not really. Here, let's find us a place to sit. Dad wants to spend some time in prayer." Storm's arms tightened around the love of his life. "I agree. God is the One who got us through this and will continue to do so. Dad? Ready for some prayer time?" Storm seated himself in his favourite chair and drew Teagan down on his knee, causing her to blush.

"That we are, son. God has been good through this. You have been hurt, both of you, but He has healed you. You have a future ahead of both of you that only God knows. This has been part of His plan.”

Davy looked up at last and studied the occupants of the room. He nodded. He had answers but still questions that they were working through.

“Davy?” Will’s voice broke into his reverie. “What can you tell Teagan and Storm?”

“A lot but there is some information that will need to stay confidential until the trials. Storm, you understand that.” Storm nodded, waiting as Davy looked down at his notes. “Teagan, you will need to testify at the trials, from what I understand. Unless they take a plea deal and I can’t see that happening.

“Why the first abduction attempt? That was Ted’s idea. He wanted to use you against his brother, Steven, to find information that he thought he had on Ted. He is deeply involved in crime in a number of cities. Steven was not. In fact, he was helping to bring in reforms to the city that would have made it easier to fight crime. That is part of what we think is why Ted came after him.

“Ted apparently thought that you had been part of the problem as he saw it. He wanted information from you that he thought you had transcribed. That was not correct, as you have stated repeatedly. Steven’s business had no criminal activity whatsoever. Ted has no remorse about the killings. He is wanted in other jurisdictions for just that sort of activity.

“The assassin is the one who tried to abduct you that day. Earl Turney, a cousin of theirs, is the assassin. He is not saying a whole lot but then we didn't expect that he would. He is wanted for abduction and murder in other jurisdictions as well. From what little he has said, you are the first one to ever get away from him in his career. He was not aware of what all Ted was after from you.

"We have gone through everything that Steven was working on and have talked with his wife. She has confirmed that she was not involved in crime. We regret that we were unable to prevent the death.

"The man who abducted you and taunted Storm? Storm, you had dealings with him when you were on the streets. He kept in the shadows but watched. You arrested family members and friends and he wanted revenge."

"Who was that?" Storm frowned for a moment.

"Jake Steers. I'm not sure if that was even discussed with you when you were knifed."

"No, I don't know that it was but then so much happened at the time." Storm stared at Will for a moment. "He's vicious. The street people always avoided him if they could. I'm so sorry, Teagan, that he had you in his hands."

Teagan just shrugged. "It's in the past now, Storm. He has to live with what he's done. I don't imagine prison will be a piece of cake for him."

"No, it won't, Teagan." Will spoke for the first time. "The attorneys are working through the charges and they are numerous. He won't be out on the streets for a long time.

"So, we were just innocent victims, in the wrong place at the wrong time?" Teagan was puzzled.

"No, not at all. Storm was targeted by Steers. You were targeted by Turney. That we know for sure. Turney has stated that you two were to be killed. That last house you were in? That's where it was to happen. Only you were to turn over everything you knew and had before that deed was done. He intended to use Storm against you, thinking that if Storm was hurt, you would cave to his demands."

Teagan snorted, causing them to all grin.

"Like that would happen. I tried to tell him that I had no information, only he didn't listen." She leaned harder on Storm. "I'm sorry, Storm."

"For what? It's not your fault." Storm raised his eyes to Will. "Will, there is something else, isn't there?"

"Yes there is, Storm. Through all of this there has been another thread. Someone standing back and watching. We have discovered who it is." Will shared a look with Davy. "Tully, Philip. Somehow someone has gone after you two and to do that they have gone after your family."

Tully and Philip shared a look, frowns on their faces.

"There has been? Who?" Tully spoke, his eyes going to Storm.

"I can't think of someone who would want to go after the two of us." Philip watched Teagan and then Storm.

"It's someone we all know. Someone from the church." Will hesitated, knowing that the two men would feel guilty.

"Who?" Storm spoke. Then, he sighed. "Brad Barton."

"Brad?" Philip's voice rose as he said the name. "But he's a trustee and deacon. What are you talking about, Storm?"

"There have multiple stories on the street that he was involved in the drug trade, to say the least. He's also rumoured to be involved in human trafficking. I suspect that's where Teagan would have ended up." Will watched with compassion as Teagan looked shocked and then her face crumbled before she hid it against Storm.

"Brad? Are you sure?" Philip didn't doubt Storm's word, but it just seemed unlike the man who they knew.

"It is, unfortunately, Philip." Davy spoke up. "We have found evidence tying him to the Turneys. He is being arrested even as we speak."

Tully wiped his hands down his face.

"This is really going to hurt, isn't it?" He looked at the rest of the families. "Have you spoken with Daniel?"

"That's where I am heading next." Will stood, his eyes on the young couple who had faced so much. "I can't tell you how much we regret what happened to you both. Storm, come see me next week. Allan and I will want to meet with you.”

“I can do that, Will. And thank you.” Storm nodded as Will turned and walked away, defeat for a moment in his stance. “Davy? What next? I know what happens but can you explain to the others?”

“I can. We continue our investigations. We present the case to the attorneys. Then, we go to court. It will take some time, but we promise to keep you updated as we go along.”

At long last, the families had made their ways home, each troubled and puzzled at the turn of events. Storm locked up the house and then hunted for Teagan, standing to watch her work away in the kitchen, cleaning up from the meal that had been shared, even though none of them had felt like eating. He moved to help her, finally holding her as she wept. He wept with her, his tears wetting her hair as hers wet his shirt.

“We’ll find someone to speak with, sweetheart. Buckley and Locklin will be the ones. I need to tell you their story but not tonight. Tonight, we need to spend our time before our Beloved Father and start the healing process.

Epilogue

Three months later, Teagan roamed the house and then moved outside to wander the outside. She had been working in the gardens, enjoying the chance to renew them and add to them. Storm was content to let her. He had simply grinned and told her that she had good ideas and he was delighted with whatever she chose to do. She had frowned at him, earning herself a long kiss.

Teagan sighed. She still had not made a decision about the job offer which she had been given. Barnabas had simply grinned at her when she told him that she was not sure and assured her that she needed to take the time. If she refused, then the board would meet and pray for another person. But for now, she was their choice and God's, but she needed to make the choice herself. No pressure, he simply stated.

Storm was back to work, but strangely discontented. The adventure, as they termed it, had changed his focus. He was praying through what he wanted to do, but he could feel the excitement building as he considered the work the Barnabas Foundation had offered him. Part of the appeal was working with Teagan. But a good portion was helping his friends on the streets. They were a burden on him.

Sam had been around, just watching and then speaking with Storm. He was ready to come in from the streets, his job to bring down the Turneys and Barton completed. Storm was glad. He had laughingly told Sam that he could have his position. Sam had simply shaken his head. He wanted to go back on patrol. The streets had his heart and this was one way that he could keep them and the people safe.

Teagan turned slightly as she felt Storm's arm around her and his kiss on her cheek. They stood for a few minutes before Storm directed their steps to the gazebo at the back of the yard. He drew her down on the swing and set it into motion with his foot. Content just to be in one another's arms, the couple sat.

"Storm? Have you made a decision yet as to what you want to do?" Teagan didn't raise her head from his shoulder.

"I'm still praying it through but that new position? It is me. It has my heart."

"That's what I'm picking up. I would like to do that too. The people of the street are wonderful. I know there are some who aren't but they always take care of me and watch out for me when I am down there. Eddy has asked about schooling and how he can go to college. He wants to be an officer."

"He does?" Storm was not surprised that Eddy had talked to Teagan. She drew them out. She didn't take anything from them but her compassion and caring had won them over. "I can see that. He would be good at that. He has a heart for justice."

"And Leo?" Teagan was worried about him.

"Leo? He's sick, Teagan, really sick. I talked to him earlier today. He has cancer and the prognosis is not good. The Barnabas Foundation has set him up in an apartment and provided care for him.

"The Foundation does such wonderful work. They really are encouragers, aren't they?"

"They are. The Foundation was built on that premise, of being encouragers and a Barnabas to others. That's what we need to be." Storm grew quiet as he contemplated what they had been through.

"Any regrets?" Teagan turned her head to watch his profile.

"Some. One of them is that I didn't get to court you, or you get to have all the bells and whistles of an engagement and planning of the wedding."

"I don't. We can do that all our lives." Teagan grew thoughtful. "We need to do something to thank everyone."

"We do. I talked to Will. What he suggested is that we make a donation to a charity as a thank you."

"We can do that. Mom actually suggested something along those lines. I said that I would talk with you."

The couple sat for a long time, enjoying the dusk as it dropped down, and the sounds of the twilight as the day creatures changed to the night creatures.

"Teagan, I just want you to know just how much I love you. My life would be empty without you in it. Even with how we met? I would have still wanted to date you."

"You would? I didn't know that."

"I would. I have seen you around town. I was at your church about six months ago and sat near you. You caught my eye, but I didn't know how to approach you."

"You were? You didn't?" Teagan snuggled closer to him. "I didn't see you there."

"I came in just as the service started and had to leave to take a call before the final song. I would have come back to see if I could speak with you but then this all happened." Storm thought about all that had happened. I regret that we faced danger."

Teagan sighed, reaching to pull his phone from his shirt pocket.

"It's Barnabas. He is just checking in on us, to see how we are. Did you know that he and Aubrey had an adventure?"

"All of the men there, all fourteen, plus Dallas and Andy, did. Some almost lost their lives. Through it all, God worked in their lives. They are stronger in their faith and stronger as couples."

"That's what Buckley said. He is a character, isn't he? But he has such a wealth of wisdom. God is using him deeply."

"He is." Storm sighed. "I guess that we need to make a decision, don't we?"

"I know what I want, but what do you want?"

"I want to be where God is leading. I gave my resignation today to Will and Allan. They are sorry to see me leave but know that where I am heading is where I need to be." Storm watched her face, seeing as Teagan took in his words.

"Then, we are agreed, aren't we?" Teagan grinned suddenly. "Are the streets ready for us?"

Storm stared at her and then broke out into laughter. He hugged her, knowing that life would be an adventure for them both. He reached for his phone, sending off a text to Barnabas that simply said "yes".

"Storm!" Teagan stared at him in shock. "He won't know what you meant."

"On the contrary, he will. I have had some good conversations with him over the last few months." He grinned again as he held up his phone for her to read. "See? He's welcoming us to the Foundation family and what a family that is."

"He is?" Teagan stared out into the darkness. "Storm, no matter what we face, given what we've gone through, we have learned that God's peace is there for us. He calms our storms for us. He allows storms and difficulties and troubles but never forsakes us."

Dear Readers

Thank you for choosing the story of Storm and his lady, Teagan. It has taken a while to write, considering the stress and difficulty I have faced as a medical office assistant in the last couple of years through this pandemic. But I persevered. It didn't help that Storm and his lady were not too forthcoming with their story. They didn't want to share what was going on. And as always, they threw in multiple characters and plot twists that I never saw coming.

Where is your peace? Do you have peace? God does not want us to not have peace. He gives it freely to us, if we ask. Christ clearly stated that He would give that to us. It is comforting to know that when we face dark and difficult times and circumstances, God is there. In the midst of the storms of life, we are not alone. We can have peace that God cares that much about us.

No matter what we face, we are not alone. That is another promise that God will not break. That has gotten me through this time of trouble and other troubles as well. That is my prayer for you.

Now for the characters who appear from other novels. The Barnabas Foundation family is found in *The Barnabas Chronicles,* all 14 of them. Dallas appears in *Dallas: Called to Return.* Abe and Emma and his team are found in the *His Guardians* series. Shay and Breckon appear in *The Hunter,* Book three of *His Dreamseekers* series Storm had appeared in Dallas' story, helping to save the love of Dallas' life,

Deri. My characters are not content just to have their stories told. They need and actually insist on being involved in other stories. I don't mind. It brings back beloved characters.

God bless each one of you.

Ronna